PRAISE FOR

KILLER CACHE

"The gang from the Hazardous Hoarding Mysteries are back for more adventures in *Killer Cache*. Hoarder Hennie Wiley's collections are as out of control as her no-good brother. And Bennington's tale, chock-full of robberies and murder, has more twists and turns that any backwoods road in Plum Springs, Kentucky."
    —HEATHER WEIDNER, author of the Pearly Girls Mysteries

"Hazardous Hoarding is by far my favorite cozy mystery series! Michelle Bennington beautifully handles very real issues with sensitivity, grace, and humor and has created characters easy to connect with and root for in this engaging mystery!"
    —CARMEN ERICKSON, author of the Fairy Taled series

"While *Killer Cache* may fall under the cozy mystery category, it's definitely a page-turner! The story takes many twists, and just when you think you've figured out who-done-it, another turn pops up that keeps you reading until the end."
    —LEAH PUGH, author of The Crystal O'Mally Mysteries

THE HAZARDOUS HOARDING MYSTERIES

KILLER CACHE

ALSO BY MICHELLE BENNINGTON

THE HAZARDOUS HOARDING MYSTERIES
Dumpster Dying

THE SMALL BATCH MYSTERIES
Devil's Kiss
Mermaid Cove
Unbridled Spirits

THE WIDOWS & SHADOWS MYSTERIES
Widow's Blush
Widow's Fire

THE HAZARDOUS HOARDING MYSTERIES

KILLER CACHE

MICHELLE
BENNINGTON

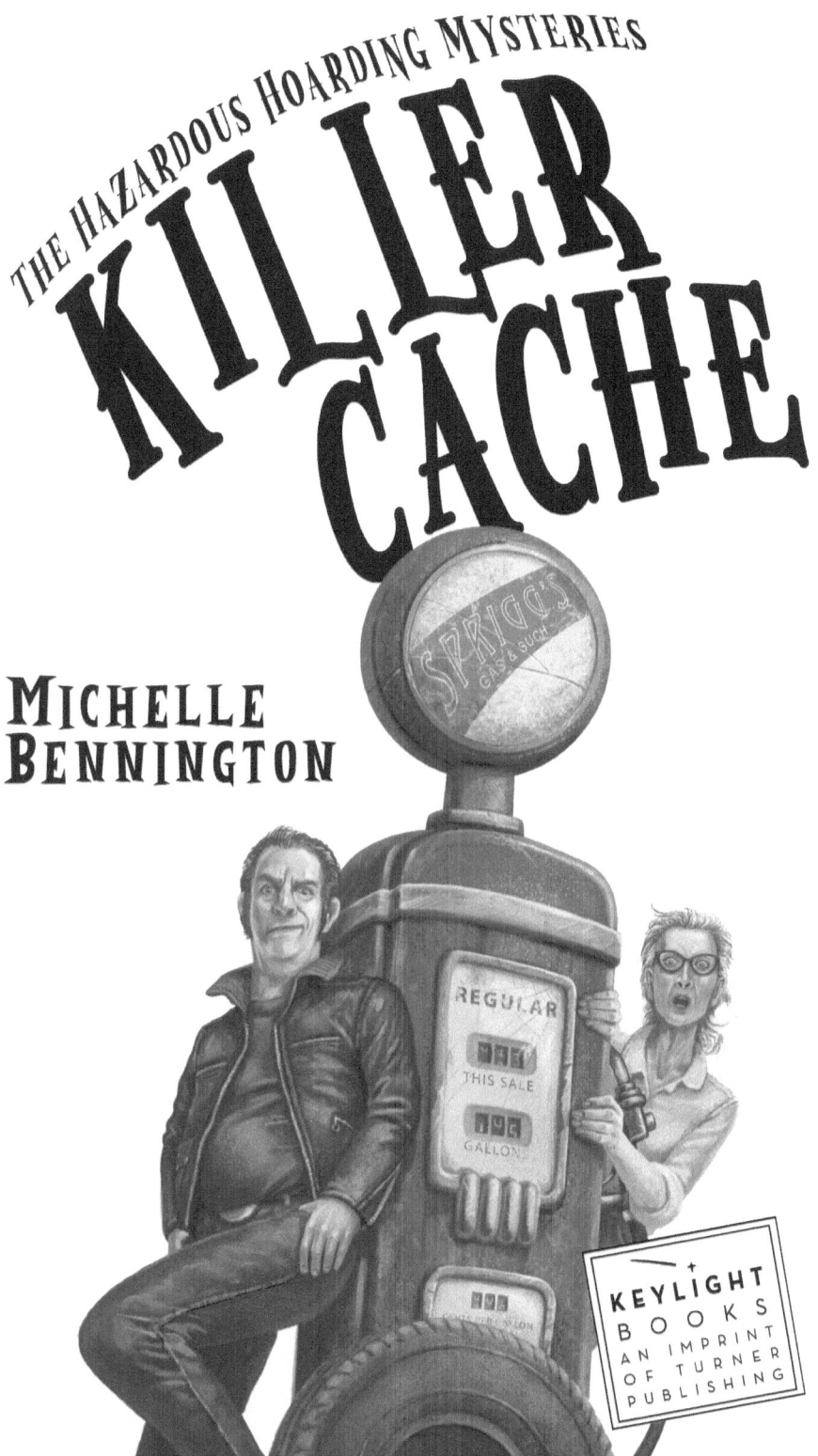

SPRIGG'S
GAS & SUCH

REGULAR

THIS SALE

GALLON

KEYLIGHT
BOOKS
AN IMPRINT
OF TURNER
PUBLISHING

KEYLIGHT BOOKS
AN IMPRINT OF TURNER PUBLISHING COMPANY
Nashville, Tennessee
www.turnerpublishing.com

Killer Cache: A Hazardous Hoarding Mystery

This is a work of fiction. All the characters and events portrayed in this book are either products of the author's imagination or are used fictitiously.

Cover design by M. Wayne Miller
www.mwaynemiller.com
Book design by William Ruoto

Library of Congress Cataloging-in-Publication Data
Names: Bennington, Michelle, author.

Title: Killer cache / by Michelle Bennington.
Description: First edition. | Nashville : Keylight Books, 2025. | Series: The hazardous hoarding mysteries ; [2]
Identifiers: LCCN 2025002235 (print) | LCCN 2025002236 (ebook) | ISBN 9798887981116 (paperback) | ISBN 9798887981123 (hardcover) | ISBN 9798887981130 (epub)
Subjects: LCSH: Hoarders—Fiction. | Murder—Investigation—Fiction. | LCGFT: Cozy mysteries. | Novels.
Classification: LCC PS3602.E474 K55 2025 (print) | LCC PS3602.E474 (ebook) | DDC 813/.6—dc23/eng/20250313
LC record available at https://lccn.loc.gov/2025002235
LC ebook record available at https://lccn.loc.gov/2025002236

Printed in the United States of America

THE HAZARDOUS HOARDING MYSTERIES

KILLER CACHE

1

Henrietta "Henny" Wiley and her elder sister, Ida Mae Puckett, returned to Henny's house, buzzing with joy after an afternoon at the Plumridge Christian Church Fall Harvest Bazaar. Best of all, Henny had won an autumn-themed dish towel set from the charity raffle and bought a super-cute Thanksgiving wreath with a quilted turkey in the center. Of course, she had at least three different autumn wreaths, but it never hurt to have one more.

"Why do you still have your Halloween decorations up?" Ida Mae asked.

Henny scanned her yard and house as she pulled into her driveway. The Halloween wreaths were still on the doors, the vinyl clings on the windows, and the plastic pumpkins, cats, ghosts, and other creatures littered the yard. The wind had blown half of them over. "Oh, leave me alone. I haven't gotten around to putting them away yet." She parked near the large oak at the back of the house.

"Better do it before the weather turns. Weather man said the frost will start setting in this weekend."

Honey-gold sunlight spread across the yard, dancing with the shadows cast by the large oak painted with autumn colors. Sadness weighed on her spirit a little at the thought of these beautiful autumn days descending into bleak winter. "All right."

Henny pulled her new wreath from the back of her sister's Buick and held it up to admire it. "I love this wreath. Minnie Wright is talented, isn't she?"

Ida Mae nodded. "Yep. Sure is. I might call her to make a Christmas wreath for me. Mine's all crumpled from storage, and the sparkles've fallen off in patches like some kind of glitter mange." She dipped into the car and removed the pumpkin pie she'd purchased from Peggy Marlow—the premier pumpkin-pie baker in all of Plumridge, Kentucky.

Henny hefted her weighty purse onto her shoulder. "You scored big with that pie."

"Yes, ma'am. Got the last one, and I'm looking forward to a big ol' chunk of this with some coffee and cream."

Henny's mouth watered at the thought of the creamy, spicy pumpkin pie. "I don't know what she puts in her pie, but it's the best thing this side of Heaven's gates. The spiced pecans on top are what make it so good, I think."

Khan, the German shepherd mix next door, was barking his fool head off, lunging against the chain holding him back, his tail wagging, his floppy ears perked.

"Does that dog ever shut up?" Ida Mae asked.

"No." Henny rolled her eyes. "Shhh!" she said to the dog as the owner, a middle-aged dumpy woman with spiky cherry-red hair, stepped out of her garage with hedge trimmers.

The neighbor, Gloria Hatfield, was wearing a black flannel shirt, shorts, and yellow Crocs. "Hush, Khan." The dog sat, and Gloria pinched off a smile. "Hey, Henny." She motioned toward the shed behind Henny's house. "I notice you've gathered a lot more stuff around your shed, and it's awfully overgrown. Perfect spot for critters to hide. You ever going to clean it up?"

Gloria wasn't wrong. There was an old tiller, some old tires, a few rusted-out barrels, milk crates, and various other things bordering the shed. Walter, Henny's late husband, had put some of the things there, but Henny still didn't have the heart to move them—even though it'd been five years since his death. "Maybe."

"I've sure killed a lot of snakes this summer."

"It's getting cooler, so you won't have to worry about snakes now." Henny pointed at her Terminix pest-control sign. "And I am pest-free, thank you very much."

"You'd better get it cleaned up, or I'll have to report you again."

Henny scowled. *So she was the one who reported me to the sheriff. Witch!*

She opened her mouth to speak, but Ida Mae stepped in. "Nosey Rosie, why don't you mind your own business?"

"Yeah! Mind your business," Henny added.

Gloria waved her hedge trimmer. "I have a right to live without vermin invading my property."

"And *I* have a right to not listen to your idiot dog bark all hours of the day and night."

"We'll see." Gloria spun with a huff, unhooked Khan from his tether, and led him into the garage.

Ida Mae studied her sister for a moment. Henny didn't like the pity she saw in Ida Mae's eyes.

"Don't pay any attention to her." Ida Mae paused, looking around the yard. "Though...it probably wouldn't hurt to clean some of the clutter up around the shed. You know, to keep yourself out of trouble."

"Oh, hush up! I don't need to think about that now."

Walter, Henny's husband, or rather his ghost, swooshed by her, close to her head. Henny tracked him. What had Walter in such a fluster?

"What's wrong?" asked Ida Mae. "What are you looking at?"

Henny needed to cover, quick. No one knew Henny could see—or hear—Walter's ghost. Not even her best friends and her sister. "Must've been a bug or something."

Walter settled near Henny. In his standard flannel shirt, bib overalls, and John Deere cap, he seethed, glowing brightly. In fact, he was about two shades shy of a neon sign. "Did you invite that flea-bitten hound dog to come here?" he said. "I don't care if he's related or not!"

Henny wanted to ask what he was talking about, but she didn't want to make Ida Mae think she'd finally gone over the edge. So, she waved wildly around her head as if to shoo away a bug, while intending to shoo away her late husband's ghost. She couldn't deal with whatever had him in a twist until Ida Mae left.

Henny rounded the corner with Ida Mae trailing behind, fumbling with her key fob to lock the car door. Henny froze. "Oh, my stars in heaven." Her mouth dropped open. Now it was plain what—rather *who*—had Walter in such a tizzy.

Cash Cooper.

There he stood on the screened-in porch, their brother, between them in age, proud as a rooster. Cash was dressed like a generic version of his namesake, Johnny Cash, in an untucked black button-down shirt pulled tight over his paunch, black jeans, and black sneakers, which were softer on his bunions than cowboy boots. Slicked with too much gel, what remained of his hair was dyed black and pushed back in a deflated pompadour.

Walter and Cash had been enemies for the last ten years of Walter's mortal life. Henny wasn't sure what had come between the men, because neither would talk about it, but it had resulted in Walter's banning Cash from the house for as long as he drew breath. And, apparently, when he had stopped drawing breath too.

"What's the matter?" Ida Mae then stopped in her tracks at Henny's side, her eyes popped open wide. "Geez Louise. I don't believe my eyes."

Cash stretched his arms wide and grinned like the cat who ate the canary. "Hey there, sisters."

Henny looked behind her to confirm the absence of a car. "How'd you get here?"

"A buddy dropped me off."

"What rathole did you just crawl out of?" Ida Mae asked.

"Now, is that any way to greet your long-lost brother?"

Henny muttered to Ida Mae, "Too bad he didn't stay lost." Then she said to him, "Why're you here, Cash? What do you want?"

"Can't I visit my family? I ain't seen y'all in ages."

Henny and Ida Mae glared at their brother. His angled smile sank downward and he pushed out a heavy sigh. "All right. My girlfriend, Sandy, kicked me out."

Ida Mae stomped her foot. "I *knew* it!"

"Dang it, Cash," Henny said. "What've you done this time?"

His voice jumped a pitch. "I don't know. I came home one day, the locks were changed, and my suitcase was on the porch."

Ida Mae threw her free hand in the air. "His whole life is a bad country song," she said to Henny. Then she turned to Cash. "Are you ever going to grow up? Don't you think it's time, now that you're in your fifties?"

Henny gritted her teeth as she charged toward the house. She wasn't going to enjoy the pumpkin pie now. She marched up the stairs to the screened back porch. "I don't want to hear it. I'm sure you did something." She put her key in the lock and opened the back door to the kitchen, flipping on the light as she stepped inside. Ida Mae followed on her heels.

Glowing white as an LED headlight, Walter filled up the doorway, pushing on Cash's chest until Walter's arms disappeared and pushed out Cash's back. "Whew," Cash shivered. "I'm cold."

Walter growled. "You can't come in, you lowdown catfish-belly."

Cash shouted from behind Henny, "I swear! I don't know what set her off this time. I would stay with my buddy Red, but, well, he ain't talking to me right now."

Henny shook her head. She propped the wreath in a nearby chair and dumped her tea towels on the countertop. She pushed back the bags and boxes on the kitchen table to make space for the pie. "I don't want to hear it."

Ida Mae snorted, setting down the pie. "Let me guess. You owe him money? Or you stole something from him? Or you sold him a lemon car?"

"None of those things. I started seeing his younger sister, Patsy, and borrowed some money from her. I plan on paying her back, though."

Henny clapped her hands. "There it is! You were cheating on Sandy and she kicked you out." She stood in the doorway, blocking his entry.

Cash lifted one shoulder with a look of feigned innocence.

Ida Mae busied herself, working around the clutter of boxes and stacks of newspapers and magazines, pulling out saucers for the pie and cups for the coffee. She took out two of each.

Sneering, Henny continued, "I knew you'd done something low and sneaky. How much money did you take from Patsy?"

"Borrowed."

"How much?"

"About five grand. Or ten."

"Geez Louise, what is wrong with you?"

Ida Mae rolled her eyes and filled the coffeemaker with grounds and water.

"Look, that was six months ago. I'm reformed now."

"Six months ago?" Henny narrowed her eyes at him. "Where have you been for the past six months?"

He paused, a look of constipation crossing his face. "Weeeellll..." Then he flashed a bright smile. The same boyish smile that had charmed many a woman out of her money or her pants. Or both. "That's an interesting story; and I think when you hear it, you'll laugh. But..." He sniffed the air. "Do I smell coffee? Whoo-wee. I shore would love a big ol' cup of coffee right about now."

Walter stood behind Henny. "He's like a stray cat. If you let him in and feed him, he'll never leave. Don't you do it, Henny."

Walter was right. "You can't come in," she said.

Cash's brown eyes expanded two sizes and drooped like a hound dog begging for a bone. His voice melted into a tender pleading. "Oh, c'mon, Sis. I've been on the road for days. Only scraps to eat. Just let me rest my weary bones for a few hours. Then I'll leave. I promise."

Henny began to soften.

"Don't listen to him!" Walter said, pushing against Henny, too. All Henny felt was a spot of cold in the center of her back. "You can't trust him."

"Please," Cash implored. "You know how Momma always said we three siblings was all we really had in the world."

Henny wasn't stupid. She knew he was leveraging her love of their parents and her desire to make them proud. But blast it if it wasn't working. He may've been lower and slimier than a slug's belly, but he was family. And family was the most important thing of all. She sighed. "All right. I'll give you some coffee and pie, then you go."

He smiled. "Thanks, Henny. You always was the sweetest sister."

"I heard that!" Ida Mae groused from inside, grabbing another plate and cup, slamming them on the countertop.

Henny stepped back to let him in.

He crossed the threshold and paused. "Holy ravioli, Sis. What's going on in here? Are you moving? Did a bomb explode?"

"No. What's that supposed to mean?" She pushed her glasses up on her snub nose and blinked, looking around.

"What's with all the boxes and bags and all this...*stuff*?" He chuckled. "Are you one of those..." He snapped his fingers to lock the word into place. "A, uh...hoarder!" He pointed at her. "You one of them hoarders or something?"

Henny's face burned and she blinked faster. She searched her space. Perhaps she had gathered a few things over the past ten years or so, but... Shame like a hot coal seared right through that tender spot between her heart and stomach. Maybe she did have a lot of stuff, but she couldn't agree with Cash and say the words. Pride, prickly and hard, clapped down over that burning coal, dousing its heat. She glared at him. "No. I'm a *collector*. I like pretty things. That's all." Even she noticed the sharp edge in her voice.

"If you say so." He closed the door behind him, shutting Walter on the outside.

Walter popped through the door and tried to pull on Cash to prevent his entrance, but his hands cut right through his arch-nemesis.

Cash dropped his suitcase beside the fridge, his gaze roaming over the room. "A lot of this stuff looks kind of like junk, if you ask me." He lifted a box. "Like this empty box." He lifted a grocery bag full of straws. "Or this. Why do you have so many straws?"

"Well, I didn't ask you." Henny snatched the items from his hands. "I need these. You mind your business, or you can leave right now."

Walter flew through the kitchen, grumbling, then vanished into the light fixture over the kitchen table. The lights flickered.

Ida Mae looked up at the light. "Did y'all see that?"

Cash asked, "Is it cold in here? Or is it just me?"

"No, it's not cold. And the lights flickered, is all. Probably a light bulb ready to blow." Henny didn't know about light bulbs, but Walter sure was ready to blow. She pushed around Cash to pour the coffee.

"Have a seat," Ida Mae said. "You want pumpkin pie?"

"Yes, ma'am." Cash sat down with a grunt. "I haven't had anything to eat since breakfast."

Ida Mae slid a large piece of pie toward him and set a place for herself and Henny. Henny carried over three cups of coffee.

They sat in awkward silence, eating their pie.

Cash spoke first. "Are things going"—he looked around the room—"okay? I mean, since Walter, you know…"

Henny sipped her coffee. "Things are fine. I've gotten along just fine." Which was sort of true. Even though Walter's body had been interred at the Plumridge Memorial Gardens for the past five years, his spirit was firmly planted on her property and, frankly, often pestered the bejeezus out of her. Yet her heart knew the man she'd loved and married wasn't really at home. It was a strange sort of limbo where she both mourned his physical absence and celebrated what scraps of him remained in spirit form.

"I always liked Walter," Cash said, taking a large bite of his pie.

Walter reappeared, sitting on top of the stove. "Lies. He wouldn't have lied to me so much if he liked me. He was more trouble than he was worth. And I don't like him." He glowed bright with anger.

Ida Mae shivered in her seat. "You know, it *is* kind of cold in here." She looked around. "Do you have a window open or something?"

Henny wanted a word with Walter anyway, so she made a show of checking. "Maybe. Let me look." She pushed back the chair, pinned Walter with her eyes, and jerked her head toward the hallway. She side-shuffled past the piles of books and boxes stacked three feet high, and the bags of empty aluminum cans— she still needed to take them to the recycling center, maybe—toward the guest bedroom.

She tried to open the door, but it caught, not allowing her to enter. She pressed harder, but no luck. Shoving against it with her shoulder, it finally opened enough to allow her to squeeze in sideways. She scanned the shelves stuffed with dolls, trinkets, *Wizard of Oz* items, and the loads of clothes, toys, boxes, shoes, pictures, and such heaped on the bed and on the floor. A narrow path cut through the treasures, revealing gray carpet below.

She touched a glittery red shoe—resting on the pile on the bed—that she'd recovered from a dumpster a few weeks ago. For a split second, warm joy lingered over the brilliant red sparkles—until she remembered it had belonged to her friend, Jenna, who had died recently.

Walter appeared on top of a stack of plastic containers, his feet dangling over the edge. "He can't stay, Henny."

"I never said anything about him staying. But you have to stop creating a ruckus. It's distracting, and you're going to make me look like a loon."

"I don't care." Walter crossed his arms. "That man is not welcome in this house. He needs to go. Now."

"He's my brother. And he's right about my parents wanting us to get along. My momma and daddy would be heartbroken if they found out us kids weren't on friendly terms. It's been ten years. It's too long for a family to not be on speaking terms. Whatever happened between y'all is none of my concern."

Walter frowned. "*Not* my problem. He leaves today."

"Why do you hate him so much?"

"Because..." He paused, and a distant, confused gaze masked his face. "Well, because..." He shifted, then rubbed his forehead.

"You want me to kick my brother out of this house, and you don't even know why?"

"There is a reason. Dang it! I can't remember!"

"How can you feel so strongly about something and not remember why?"

"Because I'm a dadburned ghost! There are big gaps in my memory."

"How?"

"I don't know how. It's my ghost amnesia. All I know is he did something to me."

"Well, if you can't remember—"

There was a knock on the door, and Ida Mae cracked it open enough to poke her head inside. "Who are you talking to?"

Henny flushed. Embarrassment tingled between her shoulders and crept up her neck as she pretended to search for something. "Uh, no one."

"I've been standing outside this room for a full minute, and it sounds like you're in quite a conversation."

"I-I-I was just talking to myself."

Amusement and concern lit Ida Mae's hazel eyes. "Ooookay."

"Having Cash here has me all bumfuzzled."

"It is a big surprise."

"I really don't want him staying here."

"Then don't let him." Ida shrugged. "It's your house."

"I can't let him stay on the street, though. Could you imagine how upset Momma and Daddy would be?"

"They aren't here. Haven't been here for years. So you don't need to worry about it."

There was a time Henny might've believed that. But Walter's presence confirmed the existence of a Great Beyond. Maybe Momma and Daddy were here too, watching. They could appear at any time to scold her. And she'd never lost the desire to make them proud. "Maybe."

"Come finish your pie." She blew out a breath. "It's really cold in here. You should have your furnace checked. It doesn't seem to be working very well."

"Yeah," Henny said, her voice and mind distant. "I might call them Monday."

When they returned to the kitchen, Cash was standing at the sink, washing his cup and saucer.

Henny eyed him suspiciously. She had never known her brother to wash a dish in all the years they'd lived together as kids. Maybe he *was* working on changing his ways. Maybe.

He sighed and turned to the sisters, drying his hands. He

tossed the towel to the side. "I guess I'd better get going. It's probably going to take me a while to find some place to lay my head tonight."

Henny and Ida Mae glanced at each other.

Cash peered out the window by the fridge. "Of course, I'm not sure where that's going to be." He turned soulful eyes to Ida Mae.

She held up her hands. "Not me. Nope. No, sir. If I brought you home, Eddie would have a raging fit."

"Eddie doesn't like me?"

"You know good and well he doesn't. Not since you"—she made air quotes with her fingers—"*fixed* his car with a used serpentine belt but charged him for a new one."

"I didn't know it was used."

"You're lying through your teeth. When the belt broke, Eddie took it to a real mechanic. He said that belt looked like it had at least 50,000 miles on it."

Cash pulled his shoulders to his ears and opened his hands. "I swear—"

"Save your breath. Eddie said if your shadow darkens our doorstep again, he'll fill your hide with buckshot."

"Where am I supposed to go? I only need a place to stay until I get back on my feet. About a week or two. Red's not speaking to me. My girlfriend's definitely not speaking to me. I wonder..." He paused. "Is there a Salvation Army shelter or something?"

Walter was the only ghost Henny could see, but that didn't stop the shrill, alarmed voice of her late mother from assaulting her mind. *Henrietta Marie Cooper. Cash may be troubled but he's your brother. How could you* dare *let him stay in a shelter? Family takes care of family.*

Walter glared at her from the top of the fridge. "Don't do it," he warned.

But the words were already coming out of her mouth. "You can stay with me."

Ida Mae snapped her head around, her mouth agape. "You can't be serious!"

Henny regretted the offer as soon as she'd made it.

Walter lit up bright and exploded like a bottle rocket into a thousand pinpoints of light. She was going to hear about this later. In fact, he was probably going to haunt her all night, every night, for the next month.

Henny said to Ida Mae, "I can't put him on the streets." And, besides, maybe there was hope for Cash—and for repairing their family.

"Well, I, uh, hate to inconvenience you. And I appreciate the offer, but..." Cash glanced around and added, hesitantly, "Are you sure you have enough space for me?"

"Sure."

"Um..." He tucked his hands into his pockets and shifted his stance. "Where would I sleep and put my things?"

Henny tipped her head. "What do you mean?"

Ida Mae and Cash exchanged glances of discomfort.

Cash chuckled. "Well, Sis, you have a lot of...stuff. There doesn't seem to be much room for a body to get around."

Henny looked at the room. She didn't see what he was talking about. Sure, she had a lot of things, collections, but it was simply a matter of organizing better. The last thing she needed was Cash judging her too. She got enough of that from Walter and Ida Mae. She scoffed and planted her hands on her hips. "How much space do you need, your majesty? You either want a place to stay or you don't. Seems to me beggars can't be choosers."

He lifted his hands in defeat. "All right. You're right. I

apologize." He picked up his suitcase. "Where can I put this? And where can I sleep?"

"You can have my bedroom."

He frowned. "I'm not taking your bed, Henny."

"Why not? I haven't slept there since Walter died."

"Then where do you sleep?"

"In the living room. In the recliner."

"You've slept in the recliner for five years?"

Embarrassment rolled over her in waves. She said, almost shouting, "Do you want the dadgum bed or not? Don't you worry about where I sleep or don't sleep." She swept past him and Ida Mae and pushed her way down the hall, opening the last door on the right.

The air was cold and stale, since Henny had rarely used the room after Walter died. She'd long ago moved all her clothes and belongings to the guest room. Which was now swamped with her collections. Boxes, bags, clothes, shoes, belts, books, and hats loaded down the bed. Yet, for all the clutter, this room was practically empty compared to the others. A bassinet sat in the corner, buried in a pile of toys and clothes Henny had acquired ages ago when she was flush with the hopes and dreams she'd once entertained for her baby, Lydia, who had died soon after her birth. She slammed that mental door shut. She didn't want to think about her little Lydia.

She flipped on the light. Dust covered the furniture, spiderwebs hugged the corners of the room, and a navy floral duvet crested the mattress. A lamp, a pack of Walter's cherry pipe tobacco, and a studio photo of Henny and Walter rested on the nightstand on Walter's side of the bed. On Henny's side was a nightstand with an alarm clock and a bottle of lotion.

Walter's ratty house shoes rested at the foot of the bed, and his plaid robe hung on the back of a chair in the corner. The closet door stood open, displaying a space filled only with Walter's things.

Cash whistled. "Looks like I'll have to do some cleaning in here. I won't be able to sleep with all this dust." He tapped his nose. "Allergies."

"Do whatever you need to do. I don't use this room anymore." With Walter and Lydia gone, she probably never would again.

2

enny sat in her truck, wearing her red and green rein-
deer pajamas, bundled in an afghan, talking on the
phone with Ida Mae. A rabbit skipped across the
frosted morning grass. "I don't know what he's doing,
Ida Mae. It's been two weeks. I thought he would've at least had
a job interview by now. Or an apartment. But all he does is sit
around in his sweatpants, eating chips and drinking Cokes."

"I told you that you'd come to regret it."

"Of course I do! I regretted it as soon as the words left my
mouth! What I want to know is how I'm supposed to get him out
of my house. He won't even do his own laundry."

"Do not tell me you're doing his laundry."

"I don't mean to or want to, but he dumps his in with mine.
Then when I call him out, he says, 'I didn't think you'd mind
since your load is so small. I figured you'd want to save the water.'
And he isn't wrong. There's no need to use so much water."

"That's why you have different load settings on the washing
machine, Henny."

Henny snapped. "I know that, but there's wear and tear!" she
huffed. "Are you going to help me, or not?"

"What can *I* do?"

"I thought you might have some ideas. I'm getting calls
from people complaining about him. Josie Marks stopped me at

church the other day to tell me how he had promised to rake her leaves for money. He didn't rake the leaves, but he kept the money. I had to pay her back."

"Good grief."

"And he keeps moving my stuff around. You know I don't like it when people mess with my stuff."

"Oh, I know all about that."

"I've got to get him out of my house. He's promised to get a job, help pay bills, and help buy groceries. He hasn't done *any* of it!" A knock sounded on her car window. Henny jumped in her seat. Cash stood in the yard wearing his robe and sweatpants. His hair stood out in a black shock all over his head, and his sockless feet were stuffed in his untied sneakers.

She opened her door. "What?"

"Are you going to the grocery?"

"No."

"We're out of syrup."

Henny rolled her eyes. He didn't have a car and she didn't want him driving hers, or she might never see it again. "Well, I'm not going out this minute."

"How else am I going to eat pancakes?"

"You know how to make pancakes?"

A crooked smile dipped on his face. "*Your* pancakes are the best I've ever eaten. I thought maybe you could make some for me."

"No. Eat cereal. Or toast. Or nothing, for all I care!" She slammed the door and locked it for good measure.

He frowned, staring at her until she turned her back on him. He knocked again.

She spun around in her seat and opened the door again, speaking in an angry staccato. "What. Do. You. Want? Can't you see I'm on the phone?"

"Why are you out here if you aren't going to the grocery?"

"Because I needed privacy!"

He lifted his chin. "Oh." He paused. "I think your house has an electrical problem. The lights and TV blink on and off all night, and the water heater didn't make any hot water for my shower."

Henny knew immediately the source of her "electrical problem." It was a Walter-the-Angry-Ghost problem. He had kept her awake the better part of the night, throwing one heckuva haunting hissy fit. She had tried to calm him down, but there was no talking to him. So, apparently, he'd caused enough of a ruckus that Cash had picked up on it too.

"Well?" Cash said.

"I'll look into it." She had no idea how she was going to smooth things over with Walter. He wasn't likely to let this go as long as Cash remained in the house. "Do you have a place to live yet? It's been two weeks."

"Not yet. I'm looking for a place today."

"Then you should get on that." She frowned. "Now go away. I'm on the phone." She shut the door and turned her back on him. A few moments later, the screened porch door slammed.

"You see what I'm dealing with?" Henny said. "If I don't get him out of my house, I might kill him."

"Kick him out!"

Guilt settled like sandbags around her shoulders. "I can't go that far. He's still kin at the end of the day."

"I forbid you to make pancakes for him."

"Lord, no. I'm not making squat for him. I'm going to change my clothes and head out to Prettie Davis's yard sale. You want to go?"

"You know I do!"

Ida Mae parked her Buick on the street in front of the red-brick Federal-style house with the rounded portico flanked with neatly trimmed shrubs. "I don't want to get trapped in the driveway," she muttered.

Several cars lined the side of the driveway, leaving an escape route for the yard-salers who milled around the tables and furniture in the front yard. Several tables laden with a variety of clothes, accessories, and household items stood outside the open garage, leading shoppers into the garage to pore over the several tables within.

Prettie Davis stood by the garage, talking with a doughy lady in a purple velvet track suit and pink curlers wrapped in a head-scarf.

Ida and Henny walked through the yard toward Prettie, who waved when she noticed them.

"Hey!" Prettie opened her thin, frail arms for an embrace. "It's so good to see y'all!" Prettie over-dressed her petite frame for every occasion. She was wearing a pair of gray wool slacks, a pink sweater, natural barely-there makeup, expensive perfume, and a perfectly fashioned bob in order to host this yard sale. "How are y'all doing? I wasn't expecting to see you today."

Henny hugged Prettie, taking in her quiet violet perfume. Prettie was the sort of woman who made everyone feel special. So, naturally, Henny had liked Prettie from the moment she met her years ago at the Plumridge Christian Church barbeque. Prettie wasn't an actual native of Plumridge, but she'd lived there for at least twenty years, so she was an honorary citizen of this tiny Kentucky town in the heart of the bluegrass region.

"We thought we'd stop for a spell," Henny said. "You know I can't resist a good yard sale."

A pearly white Mercedes pulled up and a blond woman got out, talking angrily on her cell phone. "I don't care, Jake. You'd better believe I'm going to say something. I've already made that much clear." She walked past Prettie, Henny, and Ida Mae and waved as she disappeared into the house.

"My sister Leyla," Prettie said.

"Oh, yes. I remember her. Haven't seen her in ages, though. She looks good," Henny said.

"She and her son, Luke, are living with me now," Prettie added. "They've been through so much lately."

A young woman with a lip ring poked her makeup-less face out the front door. "Miss Prettie?"

"Yes, Marcia?"

The girl stepped out onto the porch. Skinny jeans and a T-shirt with bold gothic letters spelling "Hemlock" wrapped her emaciated form. Tattoos drowned out the pale skin from the top of her pink rubber gloves to underneath her shirt sleeves on both arms and snaked around her throat. A pink skull-dotted bandeau crowned black braids. "I can't find the mop bucket."

Prettie touched her head. "Oh, yes; I'm sorry, Marcia. It's out back on the deck. I was using it the other day."

"Okay, cool." The girl slipped back into the house.

"Is that Marcia Hunter?" Henny asked.

"Yes. Why?"

"I heard she just got out of rehab. She's been in quite a bit of trouble, as I understand it."

"I know. She told me all about it. But, according to her mom, Marcia has been clean for several months and is trying to improve her life. Someone needs to help give her a fresh start, so I hired her to clean my house to help build her work history. She just finished her GED and is applying to the Frontier Nursing School to be a midwife."

"Really?" Ida Mae and Henny looked at each other, unable to suppress their shocked pleasure.

"How wonderful!" Henny clapped her hands together. "I love a story with a happy ending. I hope she's able to stay on the straight-and-narrow. I know her parents were worried sick over her."

Ida Mae nodded. "She put them through the wringer, that's for sure. Donna asked for prayers for Marcia at church every Sunday."

"Oops!" Prettie snapped her fingers. "I forgot to give her the new dusting spray. I'll be right back." Prettie jogged to the front door and disappeared inside, while Henny and Ida Mae turned to take in all the yard-sale delights.

The sisters were looking through a stack of books, debating which they had read, which they would like to read, and which ones they'd never touch, when Cash walked up.

"Hey there, sisters."

He wore a button-down shirt, jeans, and tennis shoes—all black. Cheap, citrusy—but not entirely unpleasant—cologne rolled off him.

Henny blinked. "What are *you* doing here?"

"I came to pick up Prettie's sister, Leyla."

"Pick her up? You don't even have a car," said Ida Mae.

"That's right." Henny blinked. "How'd you even get here?" She looked around for a vehicle.

He looked at them as if they had three heads. "Uh, Uber. And Leyla has a car. Duh!"

"You're not actually picking her up, then," Ida Mae said.

"ToeMAYtoe, toeMAHtoe."

"So are y'all going on an actual *date*?" Ida Mae asked.

"No need to sound so surprised. Of course Leyla and I are going on a date."

Henny glared at her brother and planted her hand on her hip. "I thought you were going to look for an apartment today."

"Leyla's going to help me."

Henny and Ida Mae locked eyes, telepathically transmitting to each other their frustration with Cash. "Maybe I should warn her to not give you any money," Henny said.

Leyla Hager, soon to be Davis again, emerged from the house. She and her son had moved in with her sister in the wake of a nasty separation from an equally nasty and allegedly violent man, Ruskin "Rusk" Hager. Leyla, with chin-length, flippy blond hair tacked into place with ample hairspray, bounded down the steps of her sister's red-brick home. She wore jeans and a white cream sweater, her makeup liberally applied with a putty knife. "Hey, Cash," she beamed, waving her hand. Prettie followed behind.

Leyla jogged across the yard to Cash with an off-white Coach purse shaped like a half-moon tucked under her arm. She greeted Henny and Ida Mae with a hug and small talk, then looped her arm with Cash's. She smelled like a mix of her powdery Chanel perfume and her spearmint gum. Diamonds and gold glittered from her ears, fingers, and wrist. Leyla's flashiness stood in stark contrast to her sister, Prettie's, understated elegance. "You ready? We'd better leave now if we're going to make the movie."

"The movies! I thought you were going to go apartment-hunting," Henny said.

"We're doing that, too. We're multi-taskers."

"When are you comin' back?" Prettie asked.

Leyla turned toward Prettie and shrugged. "I don't know."

"Call if you're going to be late," Prettie said.

"I will." She smacked her gum.

"Let's roll," Cash said. "See ya later, taters." Extracting his arm from Leyla's grasp, he snaked it around her shoulders and cast a wave at his sisters with his free hand as an afterthought. They stopped and chatted with a couple of shoppers before reaching the car.

"Between my sister and my nephew Luke, I sometimes feel like I'm running a boarding house." She chuckled dryly as she rolled her eyes. With a tight smile, Prettie turned to take someone's money for a lamp. She dropped the money in a coffee can, pushed the lid back into place with more force than was probably necessary, and turned back to the conversation.

"How is Luke?" Henny asked.

"Very well. He's at football practice right now. It's his last year to play at Plumridge High, then he's off to college."

"I hope it's not Tennessee?" Ida Mae asked, referencing the long-standing rivalry between Kentucky and Tennessee sports teams.

"No," Prettie chuckled. "Probably Georgia or Alabama."

"I can't say that's any better," Henny joked.

Prettie laughed. "To be fair, they're much stronger football schools than Kentucky." It was a truth Kentuckians hated to acknowledge. "But he's not decided. He's dating a girl, and I think he's wanting to stay close to her. Amber Knott."

Ida Mae frowned. "I don't know her family."

"They're not from around here. They moved down from Evansville, Indiana, about a year ago. I haven't met the family, but Amber seems to be a sweet girl. Of course, Luke is head over heels. Follows her around like a duck after a June bug. They've talked about going to the same college because she's a cheerleader and Kentucky has the absolute best cheerleading program. But she's a year behind him."

"Surely he won't put such a stellar opportunity on hold for a girlfriend?" Henny asked. "Are they that serious?"

Someone asked Prettie about the price of a basket. "Excuse me, ladies." She stepped away.

Henny watched Leyla and Cash finish their conversation and jump into Leyla's car. Henny and Ida Mae looked at each other, then shook their heads.

"I sure hope Ruskin ain't the jealous type," Henny muttered, picking up an angel tree-topper.

"You need to have a talk with him."

"And say what? When has anyone been able to make him do anything? He's a grown man."

"It doesn't feel right." Ida Mae shuddered. "I just know this is going to go belly-up like a dead catfish, and you're going to get caught up in the stink."

As if calling chaos into existence, a silver car pulled up, blocking Leyla's Mercedes. Leyla honked. A tanned, strappy woman dressed in yoga gear and a ball cap jumped out. She marched around to Leyla's driver's-side window and slapped it with her hands. "Hey!" Then she unleashed several ugly words in place of Leyla's name. "The next time you give advice to my daughter, I'm going to tear every bleach-blond hair from your mangy head!"

All the yard-salers turned to gape.

"What is going on?" Henny asked Prettie. "Who is that?"

"I think that's Rusk's new girlfriend, Susan Elsher." Prettie rushed toward the cars with Henny and Ida Mae on her heels.

Leyla flung open her door and jumped out. "Who do you think you're talking to, missy?"

The woman shoved Leyla's shoulders. "*You.*"

"Whoa, whoa, whoa." Prettie stepped up, waving her hands. "What's going on?"

"This witch right here told my daughter she should try out for the cheerleading team even though I told her she couldn't. Then she gave her the money to do it and signed the form. She needs to mind her own business."

"I was trying to help. She was upset and there's no reason she shouldn't try out. She's pretty and talented," Leyla screamed.

"Her grades aren't good enough, and you put your nose where it didn't belong. You have no right to interfere in my daughter's life."

"Someone has to be a mother to the girl since you're too busy mothering the wine bottle. I'm surprised you even know you have a daughter half the time."

Susan slapped Leyla.

Leyla grabbed Susan's face as Prettie stepped between them, pushing them apart. She pointed at Susan. "Get off my property right now before I call the cops."

Susan ignored her and continued shouting at Leyla. After all, petite and prim Prettie wasn't the most threatening presence.

"Jill and I are close," Leyla yelled. "And you can't stand it. She said you were being unfair and I think she's right. She's a smart girl and maybe cheerleading will be the right incentive to—"

Susan pointed, shouting back. "I mean it. You keep your mouth shut. You stay away from my daughter. Don't you ever speak to Jill again." She lifted her leg and leveled a strong side kick to the Mercedes's door, denting it.

"How *dare* you!" Leyla said, charging toward Susan as Prettie, Henny, and Ida Mae jumped between them.

"Just get out of here!" Henny yelled at Susan.

"Come near my daughter again and you'll regret it. I'll end you," Susan said as she jumped back in her car.

Leyla yelled, "I'm reporting all of this. You'll pay!"

Susan made a vulgar gesture and sped off as Leyla returned to her car.

Ida Mae turned to Henny. "You'd better get Cash out of your house as soon as you can."

3

The next morning, Henny tripped over Cash's dirty clothes piled on the bathroom floor, then discovered he'd eaten the last of the bread and bacon, which meant no breakfast. "Fine. I'll just have coffee and get something after church."

When she found the empty cream container in the fridge, she growled and slammed it down on the countertop. An irritation as dark and bitter as the coffee she was forced to drink filled her to the brim.

"That's it! I can't take it anymore. He's going today. That low-down, no-good..." She walked the narrow path from the kitchen to the hallway, muttering to herself and pushing past the boxes, bags, and stacks of papers lining the walls leading to the bedroom she'd loaned to Cash. She pushed on the door to open it as she shouted, "Cash! Pack your—" but the door jammed against something. She looked down to see a purple duffle bag with white straps. She growled and pushed the door harder, forcing the bag to roll. She froze and stared at the empty, unmade bed, the empty food wrappers on the nightstands, the discarded dirty clothes littering the floor. Her anger fizzled. He wasn't there. Where could he be? Had he left early or not come home at all?

She only pondered those questions for a moment before she said aloud, to no one, "I don't care. At least he's not bugging me right now. I'm going to Jolene's Chicken Shack for a chicken biscuit and a proper coffee." Then she shouted, "With cream!" and slammed the bedroom door.

An old familiar feeling rose up in her center, an itchiness originating in her gut that spread into her chest, into her arms and legs. She opened and closed her hands, blinked rapidly, and twitched her nose. A tightness wound her shoulders. There was only one thing to fix this feeling: a dive. No church today. There was no way she could sit in the pew and focus on a sermon when the itch to dive clawed her raw under her skin.

She normally conducted her dives in town at night. Though it was an open secret that she was a dumpster-diver, she didn't like to draw attention to that fact. But, lately, with Cash's arrival and Walter's absence, she had been struggling more and more with needing to dive during the day, at unpredictable times.

She climbed into her truck and turned right out of her driveway toward the countryside. Her white Ford pickup truck, once Walter's, climbed hills and dipped into valleys flanked by open fields, barren from the fall harvest. Broken cornstalks littered the ground like skeletons bleached in the sun. Weathered barns, their history on display, stood crooked and full of holes. At the end of the forked road emerged an ancient gas station, long ago abandoned. It was surrounded by giant farms sitting on hundreds of acres where the closest neighbor might be a mile away. Honestly, with the development going on in Lexington and surrounding towns, she was surprised that such an isolated area still existed.

Lines of grass and weeds pushed through the broken pavement. The windows were broken out, and trees and vines had overtaken the building's exterior. Two red, narrow, rusted gas tanks stood guard, deep in weeds and discarded tires.

As she pulled into the parking lot, Henny was drawn back about fifty-five years, when every Saturday she, Cash, and Ida Mae would sit in the back of her parents' olive-green wood-paneled station wagon on the way home from visiting relatives. Elmer Sprigg, the owner, would come out of the gas station, wearing bib overalls and a red ball cap, wiping his greasy hands on a rag, to lean on the window and greet her parents. Mr. Elmer filled up the tank and discussed tobacco and corn prices with Daddy. Even then the place looked old to Henny, but it was one of her favorite visits. Mr. Elmer, barely making any money at his old station, always gave Henny, Cash, and Ida Mae a cold bottle of grape soda and a piece of Bazooka Joe bubble gum from his store. She recalled the sunshine pouring in through the car window and the condensation from the bottle wetting her shirt as she and her siblings unwrapped their bubble gum with excitement to see what the comic in the wrapper said. It was a happy time when she, Cash, and Ida Mae had been young, full of life, hopes, and potential. Henny's eyes filled with tears. So many lives, so many years.

Now all was gone. Dust. She slid from her truck and pulled her walking stick and glittery messenger bag from the truck bed. She wouldn't need the stepladder or headlamp this time, because there was no dumpster, just stuff discarded by former owners. She approached the station. When Mr. Elmer had died, the station had died with him. Apparently, no one had inherited it or had any interest in the station or in his tiny white wooden Cape Cod house adjacent to the station, which was now rotted through and overgrown with brush. She knew the place had become something of a dumping ground, because she'd found some treasures in her last few visits. She'd uncovered an old Nancy Drew book, a stuffed lamb with one button-eye missing, and a birdhouse with an unglued roof.

She stepped around the rusted barrels and stacks of worn tires to the back of the building, using the stick to lift yellowed papers and bags that didn't spark her interest. She found an area where some tires had been placed around a firepit. Liquor bottles, soda and beer cans, and fast-food wrappings were scattered nearby. There were also several burned-out fireworks wrappings. Clearly this was a hangout spot for people, probably teens and young adults, with nothing better to do. The tiny town of Plumridge didn't have much to offer in the way of entertainment for lively young people. She shifted an old pizza box and found a blue rabbit's-foot keychain. She picked it up, stroked the soft fur, and dropped it into her messenger bag.

Henny continued poking. Something glinted in the grass. She bent over with a grunt and lifted out a glittery purple fake fingernail with a silver star. Though she loved the purple glitter and the shiny silver star, it would be too weird, even for her, to keep it. She thought of throwing it away, but a strange prickly feeling spread just below her skin's surface. She chewed her lip and blinked. Her free hand balled and stretched repeatedly. If she threw it away, she'd have to leave it behind. Then it would be out here alone. In the dark, in the rain. When it grew cold. The hypnotic silver star would get damaged. Her breathing increased, and her tongue darted over her dry lips. Was it getting hotter out here? She looked up at the sun glinting through the colorful treetops.

She shifted her weight from side to side. Of course, if she kept it, she wouldn't need to tell anyone. No one needed to know. Not even Ida Mae. Henny could easily hide such a little thing. The tension mounted, her muscles contracting, ratcheting tighter and tighter. Her hand hovered over her open bag, then she dropped the discarded nail into the bag. The tension in her shoulders and neck released and the itchiness in her hands and skin subsided. She blew out a sigh of relief and continued her hunt.

She turned to face the building. A wooden pallet leaned against the wall, and some cans and bottles were lined up on it. Holes speckled the building. She approached the area and found a scattering of bullet casings.

Among the bullet casings was a white paper tag. On one side was a black gun-sight target with Nate's written across it. On the other side was a handwritten code, which was nonsense to her. She dropped the tag among the rest of the clutter.

Henny studied the area. Clearly, the kids were coming out here, loading up on booze and fast food, and shooting targets. She shook her head and sighed. Liquor and guns were never a good mix, but you couldn't tell that to a bunch of rowdy kids who thought they knew everything about everything.

Henny high-stepped through the weeds and junk to the other end of the building. And there she saw it.

A car. Burned black in front. The windshield and driver's-side window were blown out, probably from the pressure of the fire. Or could be the teenagers busted out the windows. The greatest damage affected the front of the car, which was charred like a brick of charcoal in a grill. The back of the car had received less damage.

Henny's stomach twisted on itself like a nest of snakes. The car looked familiar. As she rounded the side of the vehicle, the char faded into a faint covering of soot where a lighter paint seeped through. She swiped her finger through the soot to reveal a pearly-white paint below.

No. Surely not. Maybe this was a mere coincidence. She ran to the front of the car to look for the Mercedes logo. The hood ornament wasn't there, but one had clearly been there and had been removed. She knew who this car belonged to, even as she whispered, "Please don't let this be Leyla's car." But, if this car belonged to Leyla, where was she? And if this was Leyla's car, where was Henny's brother Cash?

Henny inched closer to the car and craned her neck to peer inside. Nothing there. *Whew! Thank goodness.* She rounded to the back of the car, where a blackened cinder block sat on top of the trunk. Her stomach sank as she closed her eyes to steel herself. *Please, no.*

"Please, please, please…" she whispered to herself in some kind of broken prayer as she pulled the block off the back of the trunk. She staggered back a couple of steps with the weight of the block as the trunk popped open and a sickly sweet odor hit her nose. Carefully dropping the block on the ground so as to avoid hitting her feet, she scrunched her nose and buried it in her arm. Maybe a racoon or opossum had become trapped in the trunk? She hoped—rather than believed—that to be true. Still, in spite of her deepest fears, she forced herself to look in the trunk to confirm the truth with her own eyes.

Continuing to hold her nose, she eased forward and lifted the trunk lid, hoping to find the carcass of a critter. Instead, Henny found something far more horrific.

Henny squealed through her fingers. "Ohnoohnoohno ohnoohno." She wanted to look away but couldn't. She was frozen, her eyes locked on Leyla's dead body covered in bruises and cuts, and her cream sweater and jeans soaked in blood. She squeezed her eyes shut. A crow squawked overhead, jolting her out of her frozen state. Stumbling backwards, she clutched her collector bag and fumbled in her jeans pocket for her cell phone. But, worse, there was only *one* body. Where was Cash? Was he hurt too? Had he been dumped somewhere? Or had he been carried off to some remote location and was still alive, begging for help?

With shaking hands, she dialed 9-1-1 as she ran back to the shelter of her truck and locked herself inside the cab.

The officers came screeching into the rundown gas station with sirens wailing. Sheriff Jack Basham jumped out of his SUV. His brown hat sat on an egg-shaped head where the skin on his face folded into soft wrinkles like a shar-pei around his sharp eyes and thin mouth. He sauntered up to her truck window and hooked his thumbs over his belt.

Henny rolled down the truck window.

"Good afternoon, Mrs. Wiley." He sighed, little knots jumping in his jaw as though he chewed his annoyance like gum. "You reported a body?"

"Yep. Right over there." She pointed toward the partially burned car.

"All right. I've got the coroner on the way. While we wait, why don't you tell me what happened."

Henny watched her misshapen reflection in his mirrored sunglasses as she described her discovery. "I don't know what happened to her. All I know is I was looking around—"

"What were you looking for?"

She hesitated. Henny really didn't want him to focus on her treasure-hunting practices. Especially since he'd recently threatened to report her to Adult Services for her messy house after her neighbor, Gloria, opened her big yapper. They clearly didn't understand her hobby.

He restated his question, an edge of impatience. "What were you looking for? Why were you here in this particular place?"

"I was looking for things to add to my collection." Shame ignited her cheeks up into her hair roots.

"What collection?"

She shrugged one shoulder. "Nothing in particular. Just... things."

He nodded, a yawn of awkward silence opening between them. He seemed to be considering something. He looked around, then back at her. "How's the cleanup efforts going out at your place, Mrs. Wiley?"

"Fine," she lied. She hadn't begun any cleanup and, what's more, she had no intention of doing so. The heat of shame faded into a slow-burning anger. Who was he to tell her how to live and how to keep her house? Who did Mr. Po-lice Man think he was?

"How long have you been here?" He removed his sunglasses and tucked them in his front shirt pocket as he pulled out his notepad and pen.

"Maybe thirty minutes or so."

He nodded. There was a long pause as he jotted notes. Then he asked, "Did you see anything or anyone lurking about?"

"Nope."

"Where'd you find the body?"

Images of Leyla's empty eyes and damaged body rose in her mind, colliding with the memories of how she'd last seen Leyla—laughing, talking, vibrant. "In the trunk."

"All right. Stay here."

She watched the sheriff raise the trunk lid and stare at the contents. *Poor Prettie... Poor Leyla...and Luke! That poor child has lost his mother. He's so young.* These thoughts rolled over and over in her mind as she fingered her truck keys and listened to the crows screaming.

The sheriff placed a call and turned from the car. He sauntered, a light limp in his step. His torso was doughy with a small paunch hanging over his belt and thin arms and legs. Henny knew he wasn't nearly as frail as he seemed, though. He was notoriously tough on crime, doing his best to keep all the campaign promises he'd made to clean up crime in Plumridge and Bourbon County. Supposedly, in his three-year tenure, he'd cleaned up the streets so well that the town council had just passed the budget for an all-new jail and law complex.

He leaned on her truck. "Do you know the victim?"

"Leyla Hager. Prettie Davis's sister."

He winced, biting down on his bottom lip, with a heavy sigh. "I shore hate to hear that. I went to school with Prettie."

"Yessir." Cash popped in her mind. She hadn't seen or heard from him since yesterday. Should she tell Basham that Cash was supposed to be with Leyla and that he might be missing? She lasered her focus on the sheriff's face, the big pores, the soft, wrinkly cheeks, the hard pebble eyes looking out from pockets of skin. The tight set of his jaw. This man had seen many of the horrors humanity could offer. He looked soft, but was hard, tough, like an iron fist in a velvet glove.

She wanted her brother found. But what if he'd been involved in something, even tangentially, that might've led to this horrific scene? Maybe it would be a mistake to say anything about Cash just now. The sheriff might automatically think her brother had had something to do with Leyla's death. Cash had a certain reputation in this town that might make him more vulnerable to police suspicion. She *knew* that even her rotten-to-the-core brother would never *kill* someone. He would cheat. Lie. Weasel. Steal. Manipulate. But he would never, ever kill. Still, she wanted to speak to him first. But if Leyla had been with Cash, how had she ended up here? Dead? Maybe it was best to button her lip until she spoke to Cash first. If she could find him.

"Mrs. Wiley? Are you all right?"

Henny blinked. "Huh?"

"You went white as a ghost for a second." He narrowed his eyes. "Is there anything you want to tell me?"

"No, I...uh..." She shook her head and rubbed the tight knot forming between her eyes. She removed her glasses so she couldn't see his face and those penetrating eyes plainly. She made a show of cleaning her glasses. "I guess I'm still in shock after..." She didn't want to acknowledge Leyla's death. She didn't want to think about the grim scene. She preferred to think of Leyla like the last time she had seen her, full of life, bouncing down the steps to meet Cash with her diamonds and Coach purse. "You know." She returned her glasses to her face.

He nodded, but his squint clearly signaled his suspicion. "You're certain the victim is Leyla?"

She nodded.

He scratched the back of his head. "I didn't know her. She was a freshman when Prettie and I were seniors." He glanced up at the treetops, then at Henny. "Do you know who might've wanted to hurt her?" His gaze trickled over her face down her torso, to her hands resting in her lap, then back up.

Annoyance buzzed under her skin. He was checking her for signs of a fight. She couldn't blame him, though. He was investigating a murder, and he probably had to be suspicious of *everyone*. She softened toward him. It would be hard to live like that.

He prodded her. "Mrs. Wiley?"

She shook off her reverie. "Oh, uh. Yeah. No idea. I didn't know her very well, either. And I know almost nothing about her life. Except I heard that her husband, Ruskin Hager, was mean to her. Leyla seemed nice, though."

He leaned away from the window, craned his neck to peer in the back of Henny's truck, then returned to the window.

"Mm-hm." He nodded and removed the notepad and pen from his front chest pocket. He was old-school. He jotted a few notes. "What else?"

"Leyla and Rusk are separated, apparently. In fact, she was living with Prettie while they were going through a divorce."

He nodded again, working his mouth in thought. "Ruskin Hager. Don't believe I know him. What do you know about him?"

"Almost nothing. Only what I've heard from Prettie over the years. They met several years ago. I think he might be from St. Louis. Did something with finance. So they had lots of money." She shrugged. "Prettie never talked much about them. But then it's not like I'm besties with Prettie. We see each other at church, and we've worked together to put on different church events. Things like that. I like her, but..." She shrugged again. "You know. We aren't *close*."

"All right. Do you know where this Ruskin fella lives?"

"I think he lives in that fancy subdivision out in the county by the golf course. Paradise something."

"Paradise Grove?"

"That's it."

Basham's mouth tipped sideways as he scoffed. "Shore must be nice living out there. I'd give my eye teeth to have a home in that neighborhood. You know they got a lake with a fountain? And boat slips. It's like a resort!"

"Really?" Henny said, watching the coroner and forensics techs arrive, her spine growing weak as she slumped farther in her seat. Was this scene going to play out again in a few days or weeks if Cash was also found dead? She checked her phone. He hadn't contacted her. She glanced behind herself at the treeline. What if his body was there? Finding Leyla's body had freaked her out so much that she hadn't thought of looking around for her brother. Yet she was kind of glad she hadn't. She wouldn't be able to bear finding her dead brother. If she told Basham about Cash, he could check the brush for his body. But then, if Cash were still alive, it would put him on Basham's radar. Of course, if Cash was guilty, she wanted him to pay for it, but... She rubbed her forehead. Her head hurt. Basham was still talking. "It's amazing how the other half lives."

She glanced at Basham. He was watching her. Her cheeks grew hot. She cleared her throat. "Yeah. Not likely a life folks like us will ever experience."

A few crows argued above, and the treetop rustled with their activity. Basham looked up. "When's the last time you saw Leyla?"

The heat in Henny's cheeks flashed over her whole body as her mind raced. She didn't know how to answer this question without automatically implicating her fool brother. *Dang it, Cash! Not even two weeks after you appeared in my life, and you've already got me in a mess!*

He dropped his gaze back to her.

She would be as vague as possible. "Uh, yesterday. My sister and I went to Prettie Davis's house. She was having a yard sale."

"What was Leyla doing when you saw her?"

Henny swallowed the lump rising in her throat and licked her dry lips. "She was leaving. She was going out."

"With who?"

Henny wondered if Basham could see her shaking. She didn't want to lie to Basham, but she also didn't want to rat out her brother. At least until she spoke to him. Blood was thicker than water, right? And her daddy would roll over in his grave if she snitched on her brother without evidence of his committing an actual crime.

Basham's brows knitted. "Mrs. Wiley? Are you okay?"

"I'm fine."

"Who was Leyla going out with?"

"I'm not sure. She didn't say." Her heart sank, double-anchored with guilt and allegiance. And worse, it was clear based on the squinty look in the sheriff's eyes that he didn't believe her. She averted her gaze, unable to look him in the eye.

"Hmm," he said, nodding. The coroner walked toward them, and the sheriff shouted, "Hey, Ty, I'll be right there." He turned back to Henny. "Is there anything else you think I should know?"

"Well, you asked me if anyone else would want to hurt her..." She needed to be careful here to give details without including her brother. She knew her time was limited though. Leyla's sister, Prettie, was sure to mention Cash. But maybe this stall tactic could buy Henny enough time to find Cash and get his side of the story.

Basham lifted his brows to encourage her to continue.

"Susan Elsher, Rusk Hager's girlfriend. She attacked Leyla. Was really upset about Leyla giving advice to Susan's daughter or something."

"When and where did this fight take place?"

"Prettie Davis's house. At her yard sale yesterday." She told him what she witnessed, careful to leave out Cash's name.

He wrote down his notes and said, "Is there anything else?"

She was about to say "no" so she could get away from his piercing eyes when something occurred to her. "I just realized. The last time I saw Leyla, she had on jewelry. Diamond earrings, a gold watch, and diamond rings. And she was carrying a Coach purse. I don't recall seeing any of that on the body. But you should double-check."

He perked up and jotted down some notes. "Good to know. Would you be able to recognize any of those things if we recovered them?"

"The purse, yes. The jewelry, maybe."

"What did the purse look like?" He held his pen primed to write.

"Real distinct. Kind of an off-white color. Shaped like a half-moon. About yea big." She opened her hands to indicate about ten inches by six inches. "With a few gold links on the strap, the Coach pattern all over it."

He scribbled furiously, taking down notes. Then stabbed a period. "Thank you very much, Mrs. Wiley."

A deputy shouted at the sheriff. Basham approached the new arrivals, shouting and pointing instructions.

Henny stuck her head out the window. "Hey, Sheriff Basham. Can I go?"

He jogged back over to her. "You can go." He reached in his front shirt pocket and pulled out a business card. "You probably already have one from our last interaction, but just in case."

He meant Jenna Lawson, Henny's young friend who'd been found dead last month. She shuddered. This was shaping up to be a bad year in Plumridge.

He continued: "Let me know if you have any questions or if you happen to think of additional information."

She took the card, ran her finger along the sharp edges and corners, then tucked it in her collection bag.

"And remember, something you think is insignificant could be helpful. If you think of anything at all related to this, keep me posted. And I'll need you to provide a written statement as soon as possible."

"I'll go to the station now." *After a cup of coffee and a chicken biscuit.*

"I might have more questions. If I do, is it okay for me to swing by your house or call?"

She hesitated. Was this an excuse just to see her house? She spoke slowly. "Sure."

He nodded, a bit of humor lighting his eyes. "Good luck on the cleanup at your house." He walked away to join the coroner with a clap on his back.

Henny glared at him through her dirty windshield, which was spotted with bug guts and bird poo, as she jammed her key in the ignition. She didn't like him telling her what to do with her own property. She didn't care if he was the police. She blinked and jerked her truck into gear. It was *her* house. Her collections. Her treasures. Henny eased her truck past the array of official vehicles. She deserved pretty things. She had worked for them and had every right to keep them. She wasn't going to let some busybody sheriff tell her a dang thing.

4

enny drove down to Jolene's Chicken Shack on the corner of Denalby Street; it was a little white building with a red tiled roof and picnic tables sitting crookedly in the gravel lot. It was on the decaying side of town, which was full of empty and rusted-out warehouses, abandoned mechanics' shops, and deserted factories and office buildings. The Shack, as it was lovingly known among the locals, was a dive, but it had some of the best chicken biscuits and coffee this side of the Ohio River.

Henny blew her nose, smoothed her hair, then entered The Shack. It was a small, dimly lit space with scuffed and faded wooden floors. To the left were greasy windows, and the dark-blue walls trimmed in multi-colored Christmas lights were papered with random posters and pictures. Blues and bluegrass played from the jukebox in the back corner of the room, and teetering, mismatched chairs and tables filled the space in front of the counter. Chuck, Jolene's husband, a skinny man with a face that seemed to be made of soft leather, stepped up to the counter in his red thermal shirt, apron, and straw Panama Jack hat, which sat askew over his left eye. "Hey there. What can I get ya, hon?" His voice was deep and gravelly.

"I'd love a coffee and a Bayou Biscuit, please."

"You havin' a rough morning, hon?" he asked over his shoulder as he poured her coffee.

"You could say that. But I'll be all right." She forced a weak smile.

"I'll get that chicken to you in a minute. Jolene's out today. Got the flu. So it's just me."

"No worries. Take your time." She didn't want to go home yet.

She sat by a window, clouded with grease and grime, to watch the birds peck at discarded food as the scent of frying chicken and bacon filled the air.

She was still jittery after finding Leyla's dead body, but each sip of hot coffee helped to soothe her fired-up nerves. Before she went to the sheriff's department to give a statement, she needed to find Cash. She had to speak with him to find out what had happened last night—and to make sure he was still okay. She called the phone number he'd given her last night. No answer. But the voicemail confirmed that she at least had the right number. She tried Ida Mae's landline, but Cash didn't answer there. Maybe Ida Mae had seen him or heard from him. As if her thoughts alone had made the call, her phone buzzed and Ida Mae's name popped up on the screen.

She answered the phone in a hushed voice. "Hey."

Ida Mae was already in the conversation. "You know those pole beans I set up a couple of days ago?"

"Yeah."

"Not one of the lids sealed properly. Now I've got a huge mess of beans to eat in a very short time. You want some of them?"

"How many jars?"

"A few. I figure I'll give several people a few jars, then I'll have to eat only a few myself."

"Sure."

"Sounds good. I'll run them by."

"I'm not home right now."

"Where're you at? And why're you whispering?"

"I'm at The Shack."

"Why're you there?"

Henny slumped in her chair and rubbed her forehead. "I've had a heckuva morning."

"What happened?"

"Have you seen or heard from Cash since yesterday?"

"No. Why? What has he done?"

"Leyla's dead and he's missing."

"What? You stay put. I'm coming." She hung up before Henny could say anything else.

Chuck set a plate down in front of her and turned to help another customer with a takeout order.

Henny bit into her biscuit, and relief unfurled all through her to the tips of her fingers and toes. There was nothing better than a Bayou Biscuit. A fluffy, buttery biscuit, nearly as big as a saucer, stuffed with a hunk of fried chicken flavored with red chili pepper and apricot jam—a perfect blend of spicy and sweet. She kept one eye on the window, watching for Ida Mae's car.

Within fifteen minutes, Ida Mae whipped her car into a parking spot in front of The Shack. Henny stood to embrace her sister. Ida Mae smelled of fresh autumn air, butter, and her light floral perfume.

Ida Mae, frowning with concern, said, "Are you okay?"

"I'm fine."

Ida Mae called to Chuck for a coffee, then sat at the table. "Tell me everything."

Henny unloaded all she'd experienced.

"Oh, my stars," Ida Mae said. "You're sure it was Leyla?"

Henny shuddered. "Oh, yeah."

"I bet Prettie is beside herself right now."

"I don't know. I'm trying to give the sheriff some time to notify her before I go see her. But I really need to locate Cash to find out what happened."

"What do you mean 'locate him'?" Ida Mae thanked Chuck for the coffee and cream he placed by her elbow.

"I haven't seen him since he ran off with Leyla yesterday."

"Oh, no. I wonder to what extent he was involved."

"Exactly."

"I can't imagine what you've been through," Ida Mae said, her hazel eyes searching Henny's face.

"I'm fine. Leyla is the one who went through something. Something dreadful."

"He didn't call or anything to let you know where he was?"

"No. I'm afraid he's caught up in whatever happened to Leyla."

Ida Mae's brow wrinkled. "I'll call him." She dialed his phone. "Nothing." She shook her head and hung up. "Poor Leyla. How could someone do that to her? I sure hope Cash is okay."

"I know."

"On the way over here, I got to thinking. What about Susan Elsher? You think she might've carried out her threat to 'end' Leyla?"

Henny nodded, thinking. "Maybe. She was pretty unhinged." She twisted her paper napkin. "I wonder if Cash was there and what he might've seen. Or if he's even still alive."

"I'll try calling him again." Ida Mae pulled out her phone and dialed Cash. She listened as the phone rang, then finally shook her head and hung up. "He's still not answering."

Henny twisted the napkin tighter. "I have something else I should tell you—you know, just in case the police contact you." Henny blew out a nervous breath. "I sort of told a white lie to Sheriff Basham."

Ida Mae's eyes popped wide open. "You did *what*? Oh, Henny. What possessed you?" She covered her mouth with her hand.

Henny explained what had been going through her mind. How blood was thicker than water and how she didn't want to implicate their brother until she'd at least had a chance to speak to him.

Ida Mae squeezed her eyes shut and shook her head. "But to lie to the sheriff? Henny—"

"It wasn't a lie, really. It was, uh..."

"An omission is still a lie. Though I understand why you did it. The motive was honorable, but the action wasn't. We have to find Cash and make him clear all this up as soon as possible. And pray you don't get in trouble."

"Basham wants me to give a statement regarding what I told him today."

"Let's do that first. Leave out the part where you lied to him so at least it's not on paper. Then we'll see if we can find Cash."

They jumped in Henny's truck and headed to the sheriff's department, where Henny sat in a room by herself and wrote out a statement recalling most of what she'd told Basham earlier.

When she came out of the room, Ida Mae was sitting in the lobby, holding her purse in her lap. "I tried calling your house and Cash's phone. He's still not answering, but I left a message on his voicemail."

They stepped into the brisk autumn air. The sun shone against darkening skies, and the wind had picked up. Rain was moving in.

"Do you think the police have had a chance to notify Prettie?" Henny asked.

"Surely they have by now. Should we go see her?"

"I'd like to. I feel somehow responsible for what happened to Leyla."

Ida Mae screwed up her face. "Well, you're not. But I understand, with her connection to Cash, how you might think so."

Henny and Ida Mae pulled into Prettie's driveway as the deputies were leaving. They slid from Henny's white Ford pickup and followed the cobblestone path to the front door to ring the doorbell. A young girl, about high-school age, answered the door. She was of average height with a cheerleader's toned physique under her tight red sweater, black yoga pants, and Ugg boots. She had a sweet, mousy face, straight brown hair with bangs cut across large doe eyes, a tiny mouth, and a pert nose. She smiled to reveal crooked but white teeth. "May I help you?"

"Hi," Henny said. "I'm Henny Wiley, and this is my sister, Ida Mae. We're here to speak with Prettie. We heard about Leyla and we wanted to express our sympathy."

"I'm not sure she's ready to see anyone right now, though."

Henny flinched. She hadn't expected such resoluteness from a seemingly mild girl.

Prettie's voice came from inside. "It's okay, Amber. Let them in."

Amber stepped back and made room for Henny and Ida Mae to enter. Henny paused to take in the living room. The French Provençal style with modern touches was all some shade of white: cream walls; white curtains, opened to allow the sunlight to spill over the ivory accent rug and glint in the gilded mirror over the white marble fireplace. Pale blue and green pillows and chairs accented the room. There were only a few knickknacks and picture frames placed around. Yet, for all the sparseness of decor, the room was the perfect blend of cozy and elegant.

Henny hesitated. She was afraid to sully such a pale, delicate room. The amount of space and light was almost blinding, so different from her own home packed nearly full and dim. Her nerves sparked and her hands itched. Could she live like this? There was something inviting and exciting about this space. Something clean and open and unhindered and...*free*. Henny coiled inside herself. A sudden urge to wrap herself tightly in a blanket came over her. All this space was frightening. She felt... exposed.

Ida Mae nudged her in the back and whispered, "What are you doing? Go! So I can come inside too."

Henny stepped to the side to allow Ida Mae to enter. Ida Mae waltzed in as though she'd been in this room a dozen times. "Hi, Prettie. We are so sorry to hear about Leyla."

Henny followed, shrunken.

Prettie stood, pristine in a red sweater-dress, high-heeled leather boots, and full makeup. A tissue in her hand, she dabbed her eyes and gently blew her nose. Her nephew, Luke, Leyla's son, sat on the end of the couch, his face in his hands. He stood, wiping his wet, red face. He was tall, lean, and broad-shouldered as a quarterback ought to be. He had dirty blond hair cut short in the back with a mass of curls on top, soft brown eyes, and a few pimples splashed across his cheeks. He sniffed and wiped his face.

Amber shut the door and rushed to Luke's side, wafting a cloyingly sweet perfume in her wake. She wrapped her arm around his waist. He was at least a foot taller than her.

Henny rushed to Prettie and took her tiny hands. "I'm so, so sorry."

Prettie sniffed, her nose red and eyes puffy. "Thank you," she said in a watery voice, hugging Henny and Ida Mae.

Henny turned to Luke. "I'm sorry, son, about your momma." She patted his arm. "I know it doesn't seem like it now, but you'll get through this. You'll be okay. And I know you'll make her proud."

He nodded, tears filling his eyes, his bottom lip quivering. "Yes, ma'am."

Prettie frowned and said to Henny, "Wait. How did you know? I just found out myself."

Henny said to Prettie, "Can we speak privately, please?"

"Sure," Prettie said. Then she said to the teens, "Luke, Amber, y'all please go downstairs."

Amber took Luke's hand. "C'mon. We can watch TV for a while, to take your mind off things." She led him away, and he followed like a stray dog.

Henny looked at Prettie, trying to find the best words. She didn't want to tell her that she had been the one to find Leyla. She didn't even want to think about it herself. "There's no easy way to say this..." She wrung her hands. Suddenly the words tumbled out of her mouth. "It was me. I found her. I found Leyla, and I wish I hadn't." Well, that didn't come out right. "I mean I'm glad she was found, but I wish it hadn't been me."

New tears pooled in Prettie's eyes. She sat, locking her pleading eyes on Henny. "You found her?"

Henny nodded, wincing. "I didn't mean to. It was an accident." She sat beside her as Ida Mae sat in the nearby blue chair.

"The police didn't tell me that..." She paused, gathering herself. "In fact, they didn't tell me much, because there's now an investigation. Which means...murder."

"Right. This is such a delicate situation because…" There was no nice way to prod for information about Cash or about what Prettie might've said to the police. No way to sugar-coat anything. She just had to spit it out. "Of my brother, Cash."

"Right. Because they went out together."

"Yes. Did you happen to tell the police—"

"Of course. Why wouldn't I? I had to tell them what I knew. Cash and Leyla went out on a date."

Guilt wrenched like a knife in Henny's gut. "Right."

Prettie said, "The police didn't want to tell me when I asked, so I'll ask you. Did it look like she had suffered much?" She curled her lips inward, creating a tense line across her face.

Henny recalled Leyla's bruised and beaten body and looked down at her dry fingers. What could she say? She didn't want to blurt out the truth, but she also didn't want to lie. Prettie was bound to find out eventually. Henny picked through her mind for the best words as though they were little pieces of treasure she was pulling from a dumpster. "To be honest, it looked like she didn't go easy." It was the best way she could think of to phrase it.

Prettie melted. "Oh." She blinked rapidly. "I see."

Henny wanted to pull the conversation back to Cash, but Ida Mae interjected. "You think it was her ex? Ruskin? Or maybe his girlfriend, Susan? We all heard her threats."

"I don't know," Prettie said. "Maybe. He was awfully mean to her sometimes. And he'd become more furious when Luke refused to go live with him. It really ratcheted up the animosity in the divorce. So it's possible." She sat for a moment looking down at her hands. After a brief silence, she looked at Henny with anger glittering in her eyes. "Of course, it doesn't escape my attention that *your brother* was the last one to see her alive."

Henny and Ida Mae flinched as though Prettie had slapped them both. They glanced at each other.

Henny stammered. "I-I-I-I-uh..." This couldn't be real. Was Prettie really accusing her brother of something so vicious, so evil...? She threw up her hands defensively. "Wait a hot second. Are you actually accusing our brother of *murder*?"

"He was the last one to see her alive, as far as I know."

"As far as you know," Ida Mae said.

Prettie cut her eyes at her. She opened her mouth to say something, but Amber and Luke spilled out of the basement door into the hall. They marched through the living room.

"We're just getting something to drink," Amber said, flipping her long, shining hair over her shoulder with one hand. Her other hand linked with Luke's as she led him along. Noises of ice clinking against glass and rattling plastic issued from the kitchen.

The doorbell rang.

Prettie released a quiet huff. "Excuse me." She strode across the living room and opened the door.

A hulking man filled the doorway. He was tan with dark-blond buzzed hair and electric blue eyes. "What happened to Leyla?"

"Rusk? What are you doing here?" Prettie responded.

"I just spoke with the police. They told me Leyla's *dead*." Veins bulged in his forehead and neck, and his eyes bugged a little. "Dead? How? Why? What happened to her?"

"I don't know. Why don't you tell me?" Prettie said.

"What do you mean?" He paused. "Wait. Are you accusing me of something?" He poked his chest. "Because if you're accusing me of something, maybe you should come right on out and say it, Prettie."

"I think you know exactly what I'm saying, Rusk."

Luke and Amber came into the room, their hands loaded with sodas, chips, and peanut butter M&Ms. "Dad!" Luke ran to him and threw himself into his dad's arms.

Rusk gave him a brief, manly hug consisting of a few pats on his back, and then pulled away. "You all right, son?"

Luke nodded, wiping his eyes on his shirt sleeve.

Rusk mussed his son's hair and rested his giant hand on the kid's shoulder as he spoke to Prettie. "Can I come in?"

Prettie glanced at Luke and then stepped back, her face stoic.

"Thank you." Rusk stepped into the room and nodded a greeting at Henny and Ida Mae.

"The last time I saw Leyla was the day before yesterday," he said.

"So you say," Prettie responded. "She told me y'all had a fight. As usual."

"We did. But—"

"A particularly vicious fight, I might add."

"Granted. But—"

"I told her not to even see you. To respect the restraining order. But she wouldn't listen to me, because she insisted on going to get the rest of her jewelry."

"She took the rest of her jewelry from my house. It was hers, and I didn't try to stop her."

"What about the jewelry she was wearing? Her earrings? The bracelet and her wedding rings? You didn't ask for any of that back?"

He cast a puzzled look at her. "No. Why would I? They were gifts."

"Because the police told me there was no jewelry on her body."

"Has nothing to do with me. I didn't take her jewelry."

Prettie tipped her head in disbelief, frowning. "And I guess next you'll tell me the fight didn't happen."

"Nope." He held up his hands. "I admit one hundred percent to the fight." He wavered, a little embarrassed. "I'd had a few too many..." His voice trailed off.

Prettie scoffed. "No surprise there."

His lips pinched into a tight line. "Fair enough. I know I've got a problem, and I've been getting help for it."

"Not soon enough to keep from killing my sister, though."

"What!" Luke said. "You're accusing my dad—"

Prettie clapped her hands over her mouth and shook her head. "Oh, Luke, I'm so sorry! My emotions have gotten the better of me. Please forgive me. I'm just so upset over my sister."

Red suffused Rusk's cheeks, and he pointed his finger at her. "I did not kill her. And you'd better keep your mouth shut to the cops about your little theory."

His features grew dark. Henny shot up out of her chair, ready to pounce. She didn't care how big and strong this brute was. She'd try her best to take him down however she needed to. Glancing around, Henny made a mental note of the heavy vases in case she needed to crack him over the head. She locked eyes with Ida Mae, who nodded as if she understood the game plan. Ida Mae slipped her phone out of her jeans pocket and prepared to dial. Surely this man wouldn't be stupid enough to get rowdy with all these witnesses.

Rusk seared Henny with his electric blue gaze. He held up a hand as if to stop her with a magical force. "Calm down. I'm cool. I'm cool."

Henny planted her fists on her hips. "You'd better get a whole lot cooler a whole lot faster, mister."

"I guess I don't like being accused of murder." He blew out a breath and turned back to Prettie. "I didn't lay a hand on Leyla."

Prettie held up a scolding finger. "*That* is not exactly true, though, is it? I saw the bruises on her arms."

"I grabbed her. That's it."

Prettie tipped her head in disbelief. "Do you see how big you are compared to how small she is?" She screwed up her face. "Was." She grabbed her own upper arm. "The bruises were purple. That's how hard you grabbed her."

"I'm sorry." He opened his arms to plead with her. "I'm so, so sorry. About everything. You're right. I should've never even grabbed her arms. I'd had too much to drink and I'd been getting calls from lawyers and bill collectors that day. Trying to figure out how I was going to pay for all of it. Divorce ain't cheap. Which is what we were fighting about, because Leyla loved to spend money. As you know."

Prettie crossed her tiny arms over her bony chest and looked down at the ground. She said, quietly, "True enough."

"But I did *not* kill her. Grabbing her arms and killing her are very different things."

Luke looked between the adults, panic marking his features. "I believe him, Aunt Prettie. I don't think he did it. He wouldn't do something like that. Right, Dad?"

"Y'all should probably go downstairs and let us adults talk," Prettie said sadly.

"Not yet," Luke added. "I mean, you're accusing my dad of murder. That ain't fair. There's no proof he did anything like that."

"Thanks, son," Rusk said, defeated. "But you don't need to hear all this nonsense after just losing your mother. Listen to your aunt."

Amber perked. "What about that other guy Leyla was with?"

Rusk laser-focused on her. "What other guy?"

"The one dressed all in black."

Henny and Ida Mae exchanged a concerned glance. Henny's stomach twisted. *Nononono.* She resorted to a silent prayer. *Please, don't say it. Please, don't say it.*

Amber said it. The very thing Henny was hoping she wouldn't say. "What's-his-name. Uh, Cash Cooper."

5

Every eye in the room turned on Henny.

She blinked and pushed her glasses up on her snub nose. At a loss for words, her mind buzzed with *uuuuuuuuhhhhhhhhmmmm*. She lifted a hand. "Hold on, now. Y'all aren't seriously accusing Cash of murder, are you? He's a lot of things, but he is not a murderer."

Rusk glared at her. "*I'm* a lot of things too. But everybody sure is quick to call *me* a murderer." He strode across the floor to stand close enough for her to smell his onion-and-beer breath.

Every muscle in Henny's body screamed to step back away from this threatening man, but she refused. To step back would give this bully the thing he wanted most—to intimidate her. Nope. Her toes curled, gripping the inside of her tennis shoes as if to anchor her to the floor. She looked up at him, careful to not break eye contact.

"What was your brother doing with Leyla?"

"I don't know. They went out on a date, I guess." She shrugged. "Or that's what he called it."

The pace of his breathing picked up. "How long have they been dating?"

Henny's neck was beginning to hurt from the sharp angle. "Would you back up off of me. I can't keep looking straight up." She rubbed her neck.

Ida Mae touched Rusk's arm and directed him backward. He actually complied.

Henny continued. "I had no idea that he was dating anyone, especially Leyla. He's only been in town two weeks. And what about *your* girlfriend Susan?" She crossed her arms over her chest and gave herself a hug of sorts. "I watched her roll up in this yard and attack Leyla for talking to her daughter. That was the same day Leyla went missing, by the way, so how do we know *Susan* didn't hurt Leyla?"

He scoffed. "That's crazy! I'll be the first to admit Susan didn't like Leyla, because Leyla had a bad habit of sticking her nose in places that didn't concern her. And Susan told me about what she did. She felt bad about it afterward. She'd been a little... well...it doesn't matter. What matters is that she was with me all night last night."

"I guess you would try to protect your girlfriend. But she was unhinged. You should've seen the hissy fit she threw out in the front yard. She shoved Leyla, then kicked her car door and dented it."

Amber interjected. "I don't know how long Cash and Leyla were dating, but they seemed really cozy. Lots of, you know, PDA and stuff."

Rusk didn't acknowledge the comment but continued to glare at Henny.

Henny said, "It was their first date. If it was even actually a date. It could've been two friends hanging out, for all we know. What are you even talking about?"

Amber shrugged. "Just thinking..." she let her voice trail off.

Rusk pointed at Henny. "If your criminal brother..." he said as Henny glared back at him. "Oh, that's right, sweetheart, I know who he is. If he hadn't been in the middle, I might've been able to persuade her to come back to me."

Prettie hissed, "Never! My sister would've never gone back to you. I was doing everything in my power to keep you two separated."

They locked each other in a heated stare-down.

Prettie folded. "Of course, I never imagined she'd end up with someone like Cash Cooper." She flashed a look of apology at Henny and Ida Mae.

Unfortunately, Henny couldn't argue with that. Cash was a scoundrel. But it still hurt to have other people talk about him. He was her brother, her flesh and blood, after all. It was kind of an unwritten code in the South that a family could fight among themselves all day long, but woe be to the outsider who dared to get between them.

Prettie said, "I'm sorry, but it's true. Of course, I should've known better than to think Leyla had changed any. She always did like the bad boys."

"I'll tell you one thing." Rusk pointed his finger. "If I get my hands on Cash Cooper, I'll wring his neck."

"My brother didn't kill anyone!" Henny said.

"Dad, c'mon," Luke said. "Cash seemed like a decent guy. The police will figure it out."

Prettie stepped forward and motioned toward the door. "All right, Rusk. That's enough. I think it's time for you to leave."

He turned to Luke. "Not without my son. Luke, you need to come live with me now. Go get your things."

Distress wrinkled Luke's forehead. "B-b-but I don't want to live with you. It'll mess up my whole senior year. I'll have to switch schools and everything."

"You have no reason to stay here. Prettie is your aunt, not your mom."

"But I like it here, and I don't want my senior year messed up."

"We can make arrangements."

"You know his schooling is based on the home address," Prettie added. "And the restraining order Leyla had on you extends to Luke." She stepped in front of the boy. "You probably shouldn't even be here right now, Rusk. I've allowed it because of the circumstances, but now you need to go. Please don't make me call the police on you during this trying time." She stepped forward, pointing at the door. "Please, go now. I don't want trouble."

He paused, seeming to calculate. Then he said, "Fine. For now. But this ain't over." He turned to Henny. "You'd better tell Cash to watch his back. I'm not letting this go. If I find out he hurt her, there'll be no saving him." Prettie nudged him over the threshold of the front door and closed the door in his face.

His muffled shouts echoed outside as Henny watched him through the lace curtains. He walked backward to his car, shouting and pointing at the house.

Rusk jerked open his car door and stood there yelling at the house. Everyone inside stood frozen as if Rusk's presence held them in his gravitational pull.

Prettie wrung her hands. "Good Lord, I wish he'd just leave. He's going to make us look like a bunch of crazy people. I can't imagine what the neighbors are thinking right now."

"You mean the same neighbor who was arrested for driving his lawn mower naked last weekend?" Luke said.

"Well, he stayed in his own yard. He wasn't disturbing the peace. No one even knew he was naked until he started weed-eating."

Rusk got in his car and sped off, and it was as if the entire room exhaled.

Henny blinked rapidly; her facial tic always fired faster when she was under stress. She searched the faces looking at her with varying levels of accusation, concern, and pity. "He didn't do it," Henny blurted. "Cash, I mean. He didn't do it."

Luke broke into tears, stormed from the room, and ran down the basement stairs, slamming the door behind him. Amber started to chase after him.

Henny said, "Amber, hold on one second, please."

She paused and stood with hands clasped like she was ready to spell "onomatopoeia" for the whole school. "Yes'm."

"You said my brother Cash was here with Leyla last night?"

"Yes'm."

"And were they getting along fine when you saw them?"

Her dark eyes widened. "Oh, yes'm. They seemed to like each other, like, *a lot!*"

"What time did they come home yesterday?" Henny asked.

"They came home right before I went to bed at eight," Prettie added.

"You go to bed at eight?" Ida Mae tucked her chin in shock.

"I read until nine."

Henny flashed an annoyed glance at her sister. "Would you hush for a second?"

"Well..." Ida Mae shrugged her shoulders. "I thought it was weird to go to bed so early. She's younger than us."

Henny shook her head and rolled her eyes. "Aaany-way..."

She turned back to Amber. "What time did you see them?"

The girl looked at the ceiling to think. "Um, I guess it was about eleven or so when Luke and I came home."

"Do you happen to know what time Cash left the house?"

Her mouth tipped sideways. "I guess we all left around midnight. Leyla took me home, then said she was taking him home."

Henny tried to piece together the events like a puzzle, but she needed more pieces to complete the picture. "And how far do you live from here?"

Amber shrugged one shoulder. "Maybe ten minutes. I live over on Danbury Street."

"Oh, I know where that is," Ida Mae said. "It's over there behind the Episcopal church."

Henny ran the maze of Plumridge through her mind. "Okay. I know where you're talking about." So, Amber would've been home at about ten or fifteen after midnight. Not that she suspected Amber. After all, why on earth would a teenage girl want Leyla dead? That made no sense at all. She just needed to piece together Leyla's last movements and her timeline, to make her last hours on Earth make sense.

"You're certain she took you home first and took Cash home last?"

"Yep."

Henny frowned. Yet, Amber was also among the last people to see Leyla alive. But... She looked the girl over. She was strong because she was a cheerleader. But she was also sweet and mousy. Henny couldn't imagine that this girl would have been involved.

"There was no one else in the car with you?"

"Nope."

"Did you notice any strangers hanging around or anyone following y'all? Or can you think of anyone else who might want to hurt her?"

"Nope." She batted her large brown eyes. Then she paused. "But...I would keep an eye on the maid. I can't be one hundred percent sure, but her purse looked stuffed when she left yesterday."

"What do you mean?" Ida Mae asked.

"Are you saying Marcia might've stolen something from this house?" Prettie asked.

Amber shrugged with one shoulder. "I don't want to accuse anyone if they're innocent, but doesn't she have a drug problem?"

"Not anymore. She's been through rehab," Prettie said.

Amber screwed up her face into a smarmy smile. "Yeah, but, once an addict, always an addict. AmIright? I mean that's what the school counselor said when he did that 'Just Say No' presentation before the pep rally a couple months ago. Maybe she's using again or something." She paused.

The older women in the room glanced at each other.

Amber pointed over her shoulder with her thumb. "Can I go downstairs now and check on Luke?"

"Sure," Prettie said. "I'll be down in a minute."

Amber trotted down the hall. They listened while she closed the door and jogged down the stairs.

Prettie's face sagged and, in an instant, seemed to age about ten years. "I'm sorry, y'all, but I've got my hands full right now. I need to look after my nephew."

"We understand," Ida Mae said. "C'mon, Henny, let's go." She grabbed Henny, who dragged her feet. Henny wasn't ready to go. She still had a lot of questions.

6

When Henny arrived home, she slid out of the truck cab and shut the door. A cool wind swept past, ruffling her hair as a whistle sounded above her. She looked up into the orange-yellow-red oak leaves. Walter waved.

"Where've you been?" she asked. "I've been looking for you."

"Here in this tree." He sat on a limb, kicking his feet.

"The whole time?"

"Yep." He reached out to touch a squirrel, making it jump and skitter down the tree trunk. He laughed and slapped his knee. "Squirrel didn't know what got him."

"Can you come down here and talk to me for a minute?"

He vanished and reappeared to lie on the edge of the truck bed, hands tucked behind his head.

"Why've you been hanging out in the tree?"

"Hiding from your brother."

"Is he home?"

"No, and I'm glad for it."

"Hm." Henny frowned. "Dang it! I'm really starting to get worried about him."

"Why?"

She pursed her lips, anxious to tell him because she didn't want to hear "I told you so!" But she needed his help. Maybe he'd seen Leyla—or Cash—over on his side. She took a deep breath, then said, "There's been trouble."

"I *knew* it!" Walter hit the side of the truck, his hand sweeping through. "What did the snake do this time?"

"I don't know if he did anything. He's missing, and Prettie Davis's sister, Leyla, is dead. Murdered. There's also family jewels missing. I just hope he's alive and he comes home soon. I need to find out what he knows. Prettie, Leyla, and her son Luke need justice."

His mouth dropped open. "Murder?" He whistled. "He's a crook, no doubt, but even I don't think he murdered anyone. I'd bet my boots he stole those jewels, though."

"Have you seen Cash on your side?"

"Nope. And he'd better hope I don't." He shook his fist.

"What about Leyla?"

"Wouldn't know her if I saw her."

Henny pulled her phone out of her purse and scrolled through her pictures. "Here's a picture of her at last year's Christmas dinner at the church. She came with Prettie." She held up the phone.

He squinted and looked at the image. He shook his head. "Don't remember her." He tapped the side of his head. "Astral amnesia. But I'll look out for her."

"Astral amnesia? I thought it was ghost amnesia."

"Same thing. Astral amnesia is, I guess, what you'd call the clinical name for it."

Henny shook her head. He was living in a world she knew nothing about for sure. "If you see her, ask her who killed her. I can't let Cash get in trouble for something he didn't do."

"He's probably going to get arrested for the jewels at least."

"Not if I can convince him to return them to Prettie before he gets caught with them in his possession."

He scoffed. "Good luck with that." After a moment, he added, "I'm sorry to hear about Leyla. No doubt it owes to hanging out with your scoundrel brother."

"You just said you don't think he murdered her."

"He probably didn't. But he hangs around with criminals who would."

"Is that why you hate him so much?"

"Yep. I think because he hangs around with losers he's partly responsible for—" He stopped and blinked. "He—uh..."

"He's responsible for what?" She tipped her head.

His eyes grew large. He removed his John Deere ball cap and scratched the back of his head. "I don't know. I can't remember exactly. But I know he did it!"

"You have to do better than that." She crossed her arms. "How're you going to accuse him of something and you don't even know what it is?"

He squinted, his face strained. "I think he had something to do with what happened to me. I just can't piece it all together yet."

"What?!" She glared at him in disbelief. "That's a pretty outlandish claim."

"The longer I'm on this side, the stronger I get; and I know in time I'm going to remember what happened to me. And when I do..." He balled up his fist and punched the air. "Pow! Right in Cash's kisser."

"So far I haven't heard you actually accuse him of anything legitimate. Maybe it's all your imagination."

"Nonono. I'm telling you. I had money in my pocket. A wad of it. I know it's somehow tied to Cash. Had something to do with money and land."

"Yeah. You sold some land to help him out when he was going through a rough patch with his first wife."

"No. I'm talking about another time."

"Another time? When? What are you talking about?"

He pulled out his pipe and tobacco pouch. "He told me not to tell you. Had something to do with...with...his house or something." He packed his pipe with tobacco.

"What? Why didn't you tell me before?"

"Because I'm still trying to piece it all together. I get only snippets of memory. I don't have a memory like you do. I have... uh..." He made a rolling motion with his pipe as if he was cranking up his brain. "Imprints."

"That doesn't make any sense. If you don't have a memory, how can you talk and think at all?"

He threw his hands up. "I'm not a ghost scientist. I don't know how any of this works! Something about portals and magnetic waves and force. Geez! All I know is I got involved with Cash. It had something to do with money and...uh...uh..." He rubbed his head.

"With what?"

"My head hurts."

"I didn't think you could feel pain."

"I can't. Not exactly. It's like an imprint of pain."

After a moment, Henny said, "How much money did you give him?"

"I can't remember." He lit his pipe, puffing on it.

Henny knew there wasn't really a pipe and he wasn't really smoking it, but somehow the scent of cherry vanilla pipe tobacco filled the air around her, drawing her back to the days when Walter was alive, sitting in the recliner, smoking his pipe while he worked the newspaper crosswords and watched the news. An ache opened in her center.

"Seems like you'd remember by now. It's been five years!"

"I've got the ghost amnesia, dang it." He glowed a little brighter. "I was somewhere away from home. A big wad of money in my pocket. The next thing I remember was a big whack or something like a blast. A bright light, then darkness. Then a different kind of light and this big, powerful force like I was being sucked through a gigantic vacuum and boom! Here I am, trapped in some sort of limbo world."

"Are you saying Cash whacked you on the head and stole your money? That he *killed* you?"

"No, but...there's...something." He seemed to be straining to push out a memory.

Henny screwed up her face. "Nothing you're saying is making sense to me." She held herself tighter to stave off the chill coming from Walter and the chill from the thought that her own brother might've had something to do with Walter's death. She pushed the thought away. Too dark to think about right now. She looked down at the ground and nudged a rock with the tip of her shoe, wishing she could put her head on his shoulder, feel his arm wrap around her. That simple gesture always drained the stress right out of her in the old days.

A red truck with chrome exhaust pipes behind the cab pulled up in the drive. It looked unrealistic and impractical, like a child's toy. Henny didn't recognize the truck or the driver, and she couldn't see the passenger. "Who the Sam Hill is this? Do you know whose car this is?"

"I think I've seen that truck before." He flew toward the vehicle and, kneeling on the hood, stuck his head through the windshield, his rump in the air. He continued to push through the truck, then soon popped out the back of the cab. He reappeared in his spot, stretching out along the edge of the truck bed.

"What are you doing?" Henny asked.

"Spying. It's Cash and some other guy."

With the mention of her brother's name, relief flooded through her. *Thank heaven!*

"They were talking about getting together later. But I didn't catch the details."

"Why didn't you stay longer?"

"Too much energy in a small space. It drained my power."

She had never realized ghosts were so delicate.

"Who is he?"

He shrugged. "I don't know. He was here with Cash while you were out one day. They were in the house."

The thought of a strange man in her home, among her treasures, sent prickles of shame and anger through her. "What were they doing?"

"Making fun of all your stuff."

Henny frowned at him. "What else were they doing?" Henny peeked through Walter to monitor the red truck.

"They watched some TV. Cash went to the bathroom, then the guy..." Walter flickered. "Oh, no..." He began to fade.

"Wait! What's happening? Tell me about the guy."

"I can't. My ghost juice is running out. I'm—"

"Ghost juice? What's that? Like V8 or coffee or something?"

He was moving his mouth, but he sounded fuzzy, like a bad cellular reception. He pointed at the truck, but continued to fade. Then he popped out of sight.

Dang it!

After closing the door, Cash sauntered over to Henny, a laptop bag hung on his shoulder. The truck drove away and the driver honked.

She hugged Cash. "I'm so glad you're home. Ida Mae and I have been worried sick about you!"

He pulled back and studied her quizzically. "You all right?"

"Yes. I'm just glad you're home. Who was that?" She nodded toward the truck driving away.

"Pete Knott."

"Knott? Is he related to Luke Hager's girlfriend, Amber?"

"Yeah. I think it's her older brother. Why?"

"I was just wondering. I want to know who's coming to my house. Especially the sort of characters you might drag in."

"Calm down. He works at the Haisha Corporation. He said something about helping me get on at the factory."

"Good. I'd like to hear more about that. But, on a more urgent note...have the police spoken with you yet?"

"No." Suspicion knit his brow. "Why would they? I'm on the straight and narrow now, Sis." He swiped an X over the center of his heart to indicate *Cross my heart*.

"Well, they're probably looking for you since you were likely the last person to see Leyla...alive."

He seemed puzzled over Henny's words. Then when what she had said finally settled in, Cash said, "What?!" His eyes about popped out of their sockets and his voice shot up at least twelve pitches. "She's *dead*? When did she die? What happened to her?"

She explained how she'd found Leyla in the trunk of the burned-out car at the abandoned gas station. She poked him in the arm. "So you can bet your sweet patootie the po-lice will want to speak with you."

"But–but–but I didn't..." Cash spread his hand over his heart. "I swear it. I didn't touch her!" He paused. "Well, except for when we were making out."

"Aaah!" Henny clapped her hands over her ears. "La-la-la! I don't want to hear about any of that. Keep it to yourself."

He slapped his hands over his face and groaned. "Oh. I can't believe this." He paced in tight circles. "Nonononono..."

Henny studied him. He seemed...*sincere*. Cash had always been a good actor, as any decent con man would need to be, but he wasn't *that* good an actor. He had formed actual tears and was wiping them on his shirt sleeve as he said, "Poor Leyla. I'm so sorry. I wish I knew what happened." Then he stopped. "Wait. The po-lice don't think *I* killed her?"

"I don't know what they think. I'm just saying they'll want to speak with you because you were the last to see her."

"You low-down, mangy dirtbag!" Walter shouted from the tree as he flickered in and out.

Henny made a face to silence him.

"I didn't kill her, Henny! I swear. I've never killed so much as a mouse. You have to believe me."

"I'm not the one you need to convince. You have to convince the police. But there's more. There's also some stolen family jewels."

Cash's eyes darted.

She locked in on his reaction. *Darting eyes. Evasiveness? Or panic? Hm.* She crossed her arms over her chest. "I don't think you killed anyone. But I wouldn't doubt for a minute you stole those jewels. If you took Leyla's jewels, you'd better cough 'em up right now or I'll snatch you bald-headed."

He frowned, confused. "Way-way-wait! I didn't steal her jewels, either. I didn't even know she *had* any jewels."

"Now *that* I *don't* believe. She was wearing jewelry on your date, but there were no jewels found on her body. Whoever murdered her probably took the jewelry too. Diamond earrings, a gold bracelet, and her wedding rings."

"Okayokayokay." He held out his hands defensively. "I mean,

I noticed *those* jewels, but I didn't touch them." He held up a finger. "I wanted to, I admit that. I mean, I could really use the money. But the point is, I did *not* take them jewels."

Henny stared daggers at him.

"I swear it. Seriously. Henny, I just got out of jail. I have to be on the straight-and-narrow. If I don't, I'm breaking my probation and they'll throw me back in faster than you can blink an eye. You have to believe me, please."

"Wait. What? You got out of jail *recently*? Are you kidding me?"

"A couple weeks ago. Right before Sandy kicked me out of the house."

She groaned at the darkening sky. Rain was moving in. Fast. "What did you go to jail for this time?"

"I took Sandy's brother's car. Borrowed."

"You what?"

"I was going to return it! But I didn't have my license, so that's what I spent time for."

Henny rubbed the tight spot expanding between her eyes. "I don't even want to hear any more about it."

"Anyway, I did two months and I'm on a month probation. No big deal."

"It's *all* a big deal. Anyway..." She sighed. "My biggest concern is what happened to Leyla and her family jewelry."

"I swear. I know nothing about it. This is the first time I'm hearing anything about this."

Still flickering, Walter shouted from the tree. "He's lying! It's all that flea-bitten hound dog knows how to do!"

"I don't know..." Henny muttered. "You've made a life out of lying."

"Please," Cash whined. "You have to believe me."

Henny wanted to believe him. Desperately. "Do you know who might've wanted to hurt her?"

"Nah." He scratched his stubbled chin, and a somber air came over him. "Unless it was that Susan chick who attacked Leyla at the yard sale. She was nuts."

"What about the jewels? Who would want to steal them?"

He shook his head. "It could be anyone. I can't think of any person in particular."

"When I was at Prettie's today, she and Amber said you and Leyla were at Prettie's house last night."

"Right."

"Amber said y'all left around midnight?"

"I think so."

"Amber said Leyla took you two home."

"Well, Leyla didn't bring me home." He shifted side to side and stuck his hands in his jeans pockets. "Leyla dropped me off at a friend's house. I didn't come home last night. But she took Amber home."

"Which friend's house did you go to?"

"Bucky Henderson's."

Bucky Henderson was a fifty-some-year-old juvenile delinquent who'd been getting in trouble with Cash since they were teenagers. "Why do you still hang out with him? You can't stay on the straight-and-narrow with someone like him around. He's a bad influence. Momma always said you are who your friends are."

"Yeah, yeah. I know." He shrugged and said, "We're friends," as if that explained everything.

"Mm-hm. And if he was your friend, he wouldn't want to get you into trouble." She put a hand on her hip. "What did y'all get into?"

"Late-night poker game. I drank too much, then crashed on his couch. I lost my shirt in that game."

"You have money to gamble?"

"Nah. We worked out an I.O.U."

Henny glared at him. "Are you out of your ever-loving mind? You have no money. No job. No home. But you're out gambling?"

"It's fine. I got it under control." Cash huffed and turned toward the house. "Can I go inside now? It's kind of cold out here." A drizzle began. "And now it's raining."

Henny followed him across the yard. "Cash, I just wish for once you would be responsible. Also—"

"I *am* being responsible! I have a job interview tomorrow at the factory. I'm pretty sure I'll get it." They stepped inside the screened porch. "According to Pete, they aren't too particular about the help they hire, because they accept former convicts, parolees, and people on probation."

They stepped inside the house. It was dark, but warm. Cash flipped on the light.

"What does Haisha Corp. do?" Henny dumped her stuff on the table and headed toward the coffee machine, rubbing her chilled hands.

"They make appliance parts. Switches and stuff."

"Good. Then you can start helping pay some of the bills and buy some groceries around here. Which I hope will be soon." She dumped coffee grounds in the filter.

"Is that all you think about? Money?" He cleaned off a spot on the kitchen table and sat down, removing the laptop from the bag.

"When I have a grown man trying to mooch off of me, yes. Yes, I care about the money and the bills."

"You could sell some of this crap in the house and get some money, if you're so needy."

Irritation swept over her like the rain outside, cold and insistent. Her stuff wasn't crap, and what she did with it was none of his business. She bit down on her growing agitation. "That's not the point. The point is, if you're going to be living here, you, as a grown man and responsible adult, should feel a sense of obligation to help out instead of taking advantage of my kindness."

"We've established that I don't have money to give you." He unwound the laptop powerpack and plugged it into the wall socket behind him.

"Yet you have money for poker? And beer with your buddies?" Her face grew hotter. "It's not only about the money, Cash. Even dirt-poor, you could help with dishes, laundry, yard work. Anything to express gratitude. Decency. Responsibility."

"You're my sister, not my mom. Save the lecture."

Henny's hand itched to pull that black-dyed pompadour right out of his scalp.

"Anyway, if I get the job at Haisha Corp, the money ain't real good. I'll need every penny I can get to pay back Bucky and to save money for an apartment, so I can get out of your hair and not be such a *burden* to you."

She didn't know if she should be happy or angry. Angry that he was refusing to pay for anything while also trying to make her feel guilty or happy that he was going to leave soon. Coffee filled the air and eased the tension building in her shoulders. Maybe it was best to change the subject for now. "Where'd you get the computer?"

"I borrowed it from Bucky." He spoke while staring at the screen.

"What do you want with a computer?" She poured two cups of coffee, added cream, and placed a cup by Cash.

"Thanks," he said, sipping from the cup. "I thought the computer would help with my job and home search."

"Doesn't he need it?"

"It's an old one. He said I could use it as long as I needed to."

Henny looked over his shoulder. He was on Leyla's Facebook page.

He sighed. "I can't believe she's gone. I mean, it's so surreal. Just yesterday I was with her, talking to her, snuggling with her, and now...poof!" He snapped his fingers. "In a blink, she's gone. Life is strange, isn't it?"

"Sure is. It was like that with Walter. One minute here, the next one gone." She watched him for a reaction that might indicate guilt.

Cash nodded, clicking on a photo of Leyla that Luke had posted where all her friends and family were posting their condolences. Not a trace of guilt. Walter was probably mistaken about his own death. He did have astral amnesia, after all. Yet, Walter had seemed so certain. She couldn't let it go. She needed to know. But how could she bring it up without letting it slip that she could see Walter's ghost? She hemmed, searching for the vaguest phrasing. "Speaking of Walter. I heard a rumor..."

"Yeah?" Cash typed his own post on Leyla's memorial photo.

"That you might know something about his death. As you know, he died under mysterious circumstances..." She let her voice trail off.

Cash whipped his head around to look at her. "What? Why would I know anything about his death?"

She shrugged, and he turned back to the computer to resume typing.

"Besides," he said. "I thought his death was ruled accidental. A heart attack caused him to run off the road into the lake or something."

"That's what the coroner said, but..." She took a deep breath and released it. "I've heard some things that might indicate foul play."

"Who's telling you such stuff?" He finished his post and clicked on other pictures.

"No one in particular. Just rumors."

"Well, I think they're messing with you." He sipped his coffee. "And it's been, like, five years. Why are they talking about it now? Isn't it time to move on?" He clicked through pictures of Leyla.

His comment stung. "It's not something you just move on from, Cash. Especially when you're married as long as we were." And when your spouse's ghost still hangs around, bringing up happy but painful memories.

Cash put his chin in his hand, staring at the computer screen. "Leyla was so pretty, wasn't she? I thought I was the luckiest guy in the world that she'd even give me the time of day."

7

Henny and Cash sat in the living room, eating their supper of grilled-cheese sandwiches and tomato soup, watching *Family Feud* as the wind wailed outside, slashing the house with rain. Though she loved Stevey Harvey, she couldn't concentrate on him or the excited families battling to win money. Instead, she couldn't stop thinking about finding Leyla, the details of the scene, and the conversation she'd had with Prettie, Luke, and Amber. The things Walter had said about Cash. And how Cash *seemed* innocent enough. She looked at her brother, who sat with the computer in his lap, one hand working the machine, the other managing his sandwich.

"Your soup is going to get cold," she reminded him.

"Hm. Mm-hm." He chewed and nodded, his face lit by the computer screen.

He clearly wasn't listening. Then it occurred to her. She didn't have a computer. Because she didn't really have a need for one. "How is your computer working? Doesn't it need the inter-webs or something?" She snorted a laugh. "Unless you have some special magic computer."

He tucked his chin and focused intently on his screen, his lips moving as he read.

"Cash?"

Then snapped up his head. "Oh, yeah. I forgot to tell you. I added Internet to your cable package a few days ago."

"You did what?!" She smacked the arm of her recliner. Heat prickled under the skin of her face like thousands of fire ants stinging her. "Why would you do that?" She floundered to lock the recliner's footrest into place. "Dang it!" She jumped up. "I'm not going to pay for your Internet. You better use up all the interwebs you can, because I'm calling first thing in the morning to cancel it." She stuffed her feet into her bunny slippers and stormed into the kitchen, their little heads bobbing with her steps. She put on a kettle of water for hot cocoa, shaking with anger.

Walter sat on the kitchen table. "I'm telling you he's a menace. He's like one of them squatter people who takes over a house and you can't get them out. Like what we saw on *60 Minutes*."

Henny hadn't realized Walter was watching the TV with her that night. She didn't realize he even enjoyed watching TV anymore. She apparently had much to learn about ghosts. She hissed, "I don't need you gloating about how you were right."

Cash shouted from the living room, "You can't cancel tomorrow. It's a holiday."

She frowned and checked the calendar by the fridge. November eleventh. Veteran's Day. She growled. "Lucky for you. But you can bet your sweet patootie I'm canceling it first thing on the twelfth. So you'd better get all your searching done by then."

"Here's an apartment on Stanton Avenue," he shouted from the other room. "A studio. Looks good enough for me."

Stanton Avenue was the seedy part of town. "A perfect fit," she muttered under her breath.

She poured the boiling water over the powdered cocoa, pulled a cinnamon stick out of the cupboard, and stirred it thoroughly.

Taking a sip, her anger dissipated into little warm ripples as she made her way back to the living room.

"I hope you've got a plan to get him out," Walter said.

"Don't you worry about it," she whispered over her shoulder at him.

Walter huffed, vanishing into thin air.

"What'd you say?" Cash asked.

"Uh, nothing."

"You were saying something. 'Don't worry about it' or something. What are you talking about?"

"Oh, uh, never mind." She changed the subject by referencing the cartoony animals and farm on his computer screen. "What's that?"

"My FarmTown. I feed animals, grow crops, and construct buildings until it turns from a farm into a big city."

She smiled at the cute animals and idyllic little farm scene unfolding. For a moment she wanted to crawl inside the little village and live there herself, surrounded by the bright colors, the perfect little environment, and the rounded, sweet animals. But then another thought intruded on her fantasy. "I thought you were looking for homes."

"I was. I stopped."

"Why?"

"There's not that much of a rush, is there?"

"Yes. There is. I haven't minded you staying here for a bit, but it's already been over two weeks, and I think we're getting on each other's nerves. We'll get along much better with some space. And don't you want to have your own place? I mean, what if you want to bring a woman home? You wouldn't want your sister hanging around."

"True. Especially with all this junk taking up space."

"What junk?"

He looked at her as though she'd just sprouted an extra head. "Uhhhhh..." His eyes then darted around the room. "The boxes, the papers, the bags, the magazines, the...JUNK!" He swept his arm around the room.

Shame, searing and heavy, melted into her brain and coursed through her body like lava oozing from the mouth of a volcano. She spoke slowly, evenly, tamping down on her rising emotion. "I. Don't. Have. *Junk*. I have *collections*. Important, valuable collections. You wouldn't understand."

He pointed at a bag by the TV stand. "Oh? Is that bag of empty plastic bottles a valuable collection?" He pointed at the canvas bag full of yarn by her chair. "And all that yarn is *valuable*? Do you even know how to knit?"

She didn't know how to knit. But the yarn was pretty. A deep, dusky plum color. Probably about the color of her cheeks right now. "No." She pushed her glasses up on her nose. "But I know how to crochet. Kind of. I was going to go to the library and get a book to learn how to do it better."

"Okay. But how long has it been sitting there? Six months?"

Henny blinked at the bag of yarn. "Irrelevant. It's *my* house. And it'll sit there for twenty years, if that's what I want."

He tipped his head to the side. "And what are you going to make?"

Tears pooled in her eyes. "I don't know. I'll figure that out when I get the book. I'm guessing the book will tell me what I can do with three skeins of yarn."

He scoffed. "All right. Whatever. You're right. It can sit there forever. But should it? Don't you get tired of living under a pile of stuff like a rat in a junkyard?"

Her eyes beat out a staccato rhythm as they fought back the tears. The yarn hadn't been there that long; only... She paused and ran the time backward one year, two years... Her mouth dropped open. *Five* years. She'd gotten the yarn right before... A tear slid down her cheek as she swallowed the burning wad of tangled emotions in her throat... Right before Walter died. She frowned, confusion twisting her features. Had it really been that long? Yes.

Her mind rolled back to the day she had come bouncing home, humming and happy to begin a new project, to learn something new, excited to develop a new hobby. At the library one day, she'd learned about a charity that collected handmade baby blankets for preemies. Her daughter Lydia had been a preemie, all pink and wrinkly, before she wilted and died like a little rosebud caught in an early unexpected frost.

Then Walter died and...a fog began to descend in her skull, clouding her thoughts until her brain went numb and still. That's when, sometimes, her brain buzzed with a low, quiet anger, mixed with sadness, which began at the back of her head and grew louder, until it filled her ears and cranium. The sensation spread down into her chest and into her arms and fingers until her skin fizzled with shackled anger—an anger that could only be soothed with dumpster diving.

She spoke through pinched lips. "You're just like Ida Mae. And Walter. And the sheriff. And that nosy neighbor. Judging. Always judging. Always telling me what I should and should not do." Her voice grew louder and shriller. "Always telling me all the ways I'm wrong. Telling me I have too much stuff. Telling me my stuff isn't important. That it's just *junk*. Looking down your noses at me. Well, mister smarty pants, THIS. ISN'T. *JUNK*! It's my LIFE! And I'M. NOT. CRAZY!"

Cash's eyes glittered darkly. "Well, if *this* is your *life*, it's pretty dang sad."

"Oh, you're a fine one to talk. In and out of trouble. And jail! An embarrassment to yourself. An embarrassment to your family."

He stood. "Now you listen—"

"Shut up! Just shut up. And I'll tell you something else, mister..." She pointed her finger at him, quaking with the anger pulsing through her body. "This is *my* house. Not yours. If you don't like it, *you* can get out."

The doorbell rang. Henny and Cash froze, glaring at each other.

"You going to answer *your* door?" He sneered.

"Hold on..." Henny shouted. "I'm coming!" She pushed herself through the narrow path between the plastic containers and cardboard boxes, and jerked open the door.

Sheriff Basham.

Her anger bottomed out like removing a boiling pan from the heat. "Evening, Sheriff."

"Evening, Mrs. Wiley." Water dripped from the rim of his sheriff's hat. The rain and wind had died down. "Everything okay?" He lifted his eyebrows and pinned her with a questioning gaze.

"Yessir." She blushed a little to think Basham had heard her and her brother screaming at each other.

"May I speak with Cash?"

The witchy part of her wanted to shove her brother out the door and scream *"Haul him away now and get him out of my hair!"* But another part of her, the better part, rose up like a protective mama bear. "What's this about?"

"I want to speak with him about Leyla Hager, since he was one of the last people to see her alive."

"Well, he didn't do anything to her." She shivered against the cold air pushing against her.

"Nevertheless, I'd like to speak with him."

Henny didn't have any other recourse. She turned. "Cash, it's for you. The sheriff."

He made a face and pushed through the hoard to speak with Basham.

"I'd like to get a statement from you. Can you come down to the station?"

"I'm kind of busy right now. Looking for apartments and work."

"It won't take long. We're trying to wrap up this case as fast as possible to give her family closure and justice. You wouldn't want to be the one to snag everything up, would you?"

Henny nudged him from behind. "Go. Get it over with," she whispered.

"I don't have a car."

"I'll take you," Henny said.

Cash set his jaw, refusing to look at her.

She wasn't sure if her offer came from the witchy part or the mama-bear part, but she had to believe it would work out for the best—especially if it kept her from feeding her dumpster-diving demon and if Leyla's killer was caught.

Henny drove Cash to the sheriff's department in anguished silence sliced by the slow rhythm of the windshield wipers. They'd both said hurtful things, and neither was in the mood to apologize or make up. She focused on the road and he stared out the passenger window, arms crossed over his chest.

When they pulled up in front of the station, Henny put the truck in park. "As long as you tell the truth, you'll be fine."

He scoffed, not looking at her. "Yeah, right. That's not how it works for people like me. I have a record and a reputation. I'm going to be their suspect numero uno." He opened the door and slid out. He still wouldn't look at her. "You don't have to wait for me. I'm sure it's going to be a while."

"Call me when you're done. I'll come get you."

"Maybe I can get the sheriff to take me back. If I get to come back. But I guess if I don't come back, that'd be great for you, wouldn't it?" He cut her a pained gaze, then shut the door.

Henny watched as her brother, hands in pockets, head lowered against the cold wind and mist, walked across the parking lot alone.

Henny returned home, driving past store after store, all preparing to close for the evening. The Ladybug Consignment shop, the Hobby Hut, the Luxe Locks Salon—all the best dumpsters like sirens calling out to her, attempting to lure her into their dark maws. She could almost hear their whispery silvered tones: *Heeennnny! Heeeeennnny! Come to us. Come inside. Find your treasures. So many treasures.* She wanted desperately to heed their voices, to dive into the nearest dumpster and dig for delights for the rest of the night. It would most assuredly take the edge off her nerves right now.

But after her argument with Cash, the judgment he'd leveled at her, shame sat on her like a vulture. Even if she tried to dumpster-dive, she wouldn't enjoy it. In fact, ever since Cash moved in, she'd battled this constant emotional tug-of-war between desire and shame. She white-knuckled the steering wheel and popped in a CD. It just had to be Johnny Cash's "Ring of Fire" from her Country's Greatest Hits album. *I fell into a burning ring of fire...* Nope.

"I'm already in my own burning ring of fire, Johnny," she muttered, ejecting the CD. She pressed harder on the gas pedal. She just needed to be home. Now.

Once she arrived home, she paced the kitchen like a caged tiger, crunching on orange cheese puffs. She wasn't hungry, but the crunch of the snacks gave her something to do and helped to drown out the thoughts of treasure-hunting looping in her mind. She wanted to help Cash. She wanted him out of her house. She wanted her life back. She wanted to dumpster-dive. She wanted to *not* dumpster-dive. She wanted a spacious, bright living room like Prettie's—but was afraid.

Most of all, she wanted her brother to be innocent. She wanted him out of Sheriff Basham's sights. She wanted Prettie to have her jewels back and for Leyla's murder to be solved. But who could be to blame for it? Right now, Cash, Rusk the ex-husband, and Rusk's girlfriend, Susan, were the most obvious suspects. She had seen a ton of *Forensic Files* where husbands killed their wives to remove the financial obstacle of a messy divorce and to be free to date someone else. So, it wasn't out of the realm of possibility. After all, Rusk was an angry, violent man. And Leyla had a re-straining order against him. His girlfriend, Susan, was also angry and violent. Susan had proven her violent nature when she at-tacked Leyla in front of a bunch of people. Surely, the police were investigating Rusk and Susan too. Maybe interviewing Cash was just a formality and the police were trying to be thorough.

However, as far as Henny knew, Cash was the only one with a record. No doubt his past and his reputation would move him up the suspect list for the police. He was an easy target. Maybe there was someone else? She didn't really know enough about Leyla to know if any other unsavory folks littered her life. One thing was certain: with a failed marriage to Rusk and a date with Cash, Leyla liked the bad-boy type.

She licked the orange dust off her fingers, washed her hands, and checked the time. Nine. It was too late to call Prettie now. She'd already be in bed. But first thing in the morning, Henny was going over to Prettie's house to dig for more information. Cash might be an aggravating pain in the backside with a questionable past, but if he was innocent, he deserved justice too.

8

enny batted open her eyes to some infernal racket in her house. Her mind foggy from interrupted sleep, she grasped at her surroundings. She was stretched out in her recliner, only one bunny slipper on, a ball of yarn in her lap, and a crochet hook in her hand. Cash's laptop sat on the table beside her. Too wired to sleep last night, she had tried to teach herself to crochet from the Internet. A YouTube commercial about some natural constipation aid shouted at her. She looked down at the line of yarn that she had managed to form into crooked and twisted links. This crochet-learning thing was going to take some time. The pounding continued.

She shouted at the ceiling. "Walter, are you making all that blasted noise?" On the next round of thumps, she realized someone was knocking at the kitchen door. "I'm coming!" she shouted, scrambling to lower the stubborn footrest on the recliner.

Stiff, she made her way to the kitchen door and peeked out the curtain. Ida Mae scowled back, red-faced, a box in her hands. She yelled. "Open the dadburned door!"

Henny unlocked the door and opened it wide, letting in a stiff, cold breeze.

Ida Mae barreled inside. "Watch out. It's heavy," she puffed, placing the box on the kitchen table.

"What's this?"

"Those green beans I told you about."

"Good Lord! What am I going to do with all those jars?" Henny peered into the box. "I wouldn't be able to eat that many green beans if I had twenty years to do it. Why'd you make so many?"

"Had a good crop and I couldn't throw them away. Just take what you want and give the rest away." She turned to get a cup of coffee. "No coffee?"

"I just woke up."

Ida Mae put a new filter in the coffee machine. "Did you speak to Cash yet?"

"Oh yeah." Henny told her sister everything: how Cash insisted he was innocent, how he'd recently been arrested and was on probation for a Class B misdemeanor, how they'd had an intense argument, and how he'd been questioned by the police last night.

Ida Mae poured two cups of coffee and handed one to Henny. "I don't know if he'll ever straighten out."

Henny took a long drag from her coffee cup. "I just remembered. He never called for me to pick him up last night." She pushed through the narrow hall and opened Cash's bedroom door. He wasn't there. *Oh, no!* Was he sitting in some jail cell now? She sidestepped rapidly down the hall and returned to the kitchen. She grabbed the phone and took another drink of coffee. "He's not in his room. I don't think he came home last night." She dialed the station and asked for Sheriff Basham.

When he answered, she said, "Hi. This is Henny Wiley. You interviewed my brother, Cash, last night. Did you happen to bring him home when y'all were done? Or is he in jail?"

"I didn't bring him home. I offered, but he said he was going to call a friend to come get him."

"Do you know who picked him up?"

"No, ma'am."

"What time did he leave?"

"Probably around midnight or so."

"Wow. That was a long interview."

"We had a lot to cover."

"Like what? Have you found any evidence against him?"

"Ma'am, I can't discuss information which might affect the investigation."

Henny knew that, but figured it couldn't hurt to ask.

"Is there anything else I can help you with, Mrs. Wiley?"

"No, sir. Thank you." Henny hung up and blew out a breath. She shared what she'd learned with Ida Mae.

"I'm sure he'll come back soon. He was probably still upset after your argument and the police interview. He's probably hanging out with friends."

Henny sipped her coffee. "I guess. I'm not sure he should be hanging out with some of those so-called friends."

"Amen, sister."

"Speaking of which, I want to go to Prettie's house and see if we can find out more. Maybe we can help Cash. I'm afraid with his background, the police might've already made up their minds that he's the killer."

"What do you mean *we*?" Ida Mae said with a sparkle in her eyes.

"Well...you're here. I figured you might want to come along with me."

"I was teasing. Let's roll!"

Prettie answered her door. She was dressed in a black turtleneck and black pants. Her face pale and drawn, she squinted against the sunny day. "Hey, Henny. Ida Mae." Her voice sounded weak.

Henny tried to tuck her fluffy, short hair behind her ears, though the wind kept blowing it around. "Hey, Prettie. We're sorry to bother you. Can we talk for a minute?"

"About what?"

"About your sister. And Cash."

She stepped back. "C'mon in."

"We won't keep you long," Ida Mae said. They all sat down in the bright, spacious living room. Henny balled up inside herself, hiding from the openness.

"The police have been talking to my brother. I really don't think he had anything to do with Leyla's death. Can you think of anyone else who would want her dead? I mean, it wouldn't surprise me if he took the jewelry. I will admit that. But I know he isn't a murderer. There must be someone..."

"I don't know what to tell you, Henny," Prettie said, crossing her legs, looking like a little girl in the plush, extra wide chair. "As far as we all know, Cash was the last one to see Leyla alive. You should also know, by the way, I still haven't found the jewelry Leyla collected from Ruskin."

Granted. That sounded a lot more like Cash's M.O. *Modus Operandi*—a phrase Henny had recently learned on *Dateline*. She said, "Is it possible your maid might've stolen the jewels? I mean, she's a recovering addict."

Prettie cocked an eyebrow. "Or maybe Cash killed Leyla for the jewelry. Maybe he tried to take them, she caught him, they fought, and he killed her accidentally. That's the thought which kept me awake all last night."

Henny hadn't thought of that.

Ida Mae interjected. "But Henny brings up a good point, Prettie. Amber had also mentioned your maid, Marcia, as a possibility."

Prettie frowned, shaking her head. "No. I don't think so. She seems clean to me. She speaks clearly, her eyes and demeanor are alert and clear, not lethargic or sluggish or erratic." She paused. "I don't know. I guess it's possible she might've stolen the jewelry, but then what about the murder? How? Why? She wasn't here when Leyla and Cash returned after the movie."

"Or what about Susan, Rusk's girlfriend?" Henny said.

Prettie hesitated. "I suppose it's possible."

"Does she live around here?" Ida Mae asked.

"She lives over on Bellevue Avenue."

Henny snorted a laugh. "That sounds appropriate after her crazy display."

Ida Mae giggled behind her hand. Prettie pressed her lips into a tight smile and continued: "She lives in the white house with black trim. I guess you're going to go talk to her?"

"Maybe. I'd like to see if we can find out something," Henny said.

Prettie shook her head. "Probably not a good idea. She gets mean when she drinks. As I understand it, she drinks a lot. Might be best to leave it to the police."

"What sort of jewelry are you missing?" Ida Mae asked. "Can you describe it?"

"It was our family jewelry passed down for generations. Also, there was stuff Rusk had given her during their marriage. The wedding ring, bracelets, earrings. Mostly diamonds. All of which she wore on her date with Cash. But Rusk had also given her a pearl necklace and earring set and a full set of emerald jewelry, since emeralds were her favorite. That included a pair of dangling earrings, a solitaire necklace, a ring surrounded by pearls and diamonds, and a matching bracelet. She loved those emeralds. She wore them all the time."

Henny said, "Maybe she had them and misplaced them. Or—"

"No." Prettie cut her hands through the air. "She specifically told me she was going to Rusk's to get them. He had them locked in the safe with his guns, and he had changed the combination when she left him, which is why she couldn't get them when he wasn't home."

"I still think he might've done it," Henny said. "We were here when he came by and saw how he acted. We all know he's jealous and violent. Maybe he saw her with Cash and he snapped."

Prettie deflated, dipping her head between her hunched, bony shoulders, wringing her hands. She grabbed a hand of each sister. "I don't know what I'm going to do. Leyla's gone. Died a horrible death. And now I have Luke to tend to. For however long he can stay. I'm sure Rusk will drag us all into court. And all of Leyla's funeral arrangements. I-I-I'm just...*lost.*"

"Oh, sugar," Ida Mae said, scooching forward to the edge of her chair and reaching to pat Prettie's knee. "We're so sorry you have to go through all this."

"Please don't hate me for suspecting Cash." Prettie pulled a fresh tissue from the box on the coffee table and blew her nose.

"Of course we don't hate you," Henny said. "It's completely normal to suspect him since they'd been in each other's company so close to her death."

Ida Mae added, "And with his past..." She let her voice trail off.

Prettie's watery gaze locked on Henny's face. "Who killed my sister? I have to know."

Henny's heart wrung like a dishrag in her chest. She liked Prettie, and she hated to see anyone suffer. Sympathy tears filled her eyes. She wanted only to help her friend find peace and calm—while keeping her brother, Cash, out of jail. "I wonder if there was anyone else who might've wanted to kill her. There must be someone or something we're overlooking."

Prettie sighed heavily and gazed upward, thinking.

"Maybe someone she'd had a disagreement with lately?" Ida Mae said.

Prettie slapped her knee. "Oh! Why didn't I think of him before? I'm such a mess. There is someone she had a huge falling-out with. His name is uh...uh..." She closed her eyes and pressed the middle of her forehead. "I hate menopause brain. Jake...Jake..." She paused. "It's right on the tip of my tongue. Jake Arnold!"

"Who's that?" Henny said.

"He's one of the realtors who works in her firm. Apparently, they'd had a huge blowout, but she never told me what the issue was. She was on her way out of the house; and then by the time she'd returned, I'd forgotten all about it."

"Have you told the police yet?" Henny asked.

"No. I'd forgotten to mention it in my initial interview with them. I've been so distracted and worried. I'm afraid Rusk might try something since he wants Luke back and Luke doesn't want to go."

"You need to tell the police about Jake Arnold," Ida Mae said.

"Yes. And your fears about Rusk taking Luke," Henny added.

"I will as soon as we're done here."

Henny screwed up her mouth in thought. Maybe she could talk to Jake Arnold and get a read on him. "Hm. What firm did Leyla work at?"

"Altamonte Realtors. That big brown brick building on Owensboro Avenue, across from the Plumridge Credit Union."

"Oh, yeah. I know where it is," Ida Mae said, nodding.

Prettie frowned. "I can't imagine what kind of argument between co-workers could make one kill the other."

Henny nodded. "Good point. Either you're wrong about this Jake guy, or she found some big-time dirt on him."

Prettie wilted. She seemed to age about ten years before Henny's eyes. "I hope the police find out something soon. I can't be at peace until I know who killed my sister. And I know Luke feels the same. He needs closure about his mom." Her voice grew watery, and she blew her nose. "What are we going to do?"

The words jumped from Henny's mouth before she could stop them. "I don't know, but I'm going to do my best to find out."

9

As they left the house, Ida Mae followed Henny across the yard, grousing. "What on earth do you think you're going to do to help find Leyla's killer? Why would you even promise such a thing?"

"I don't know yet. But I can't stand to see a friend suffer."

"Okay. You give her a hug. Bake her a cake or take her a gift. You don't promise to hunt down a crazed killer!"

"It wasn't a promise, exactly; it was—"

"It was you losing your mind. That's what it was."

Henny stopped and spun on her sister. "I don't want to hear it. I've already said it." She swiped her hand wildly through the air. "It's already out there. So now I'm obligated."

Ida Mae huffed. "You aren't obligated to do squat. I think Prettie will understand if you don't actually put your life on the line to find a killer."

"This isn't just about Prettie and Leyla," Henny hissed. "Don't you get it? This is about our own flesh and blood. This is about Cash. I can't let him go down for something he didn't do. Momma and Daddy would be devastated if we let that happen to him."

"Cash is a grown man, and Momma and Daddy are dead."

Henny pointed between herself and her sister. "We, and Cash, are all we have. That's it. We don't have kids. You're the only one with a spouse. We have no other family. This is it. And I'll eat broken glass before I let anything happen to you or Cash. You two are all I have left. We. Are. *Family.* And family is all there is. Yes, he's a scoundrel and a weasel. Yes, we can't trust him. But we can't give up on him. He's our brother, Ida Mae. So, you do what you want. I'm doing this."

Ida Mae shook her head. "Sometimes you have more heart than sense. But I guess that's what makes you...you."

"Whatever."

Henny and Ida Mae climbed into Henny's truck. Henny put her keys in the ignition and sat behind the wheel, staring at the house. She rubbed her face, her cheeks soft and squishy against her palms like wads of bread dough.

"So now what?" Ida Mae asked.

"I'm going to go talk to Jake Arnold. And maybe Ruskin's girlfriend, Susan."

"Seriously?"

Henny gazed at the flecks of splattered bugs on the windshield, rolling possibilities through her mind. Her thoughts spilled out. "Yep. I've got to start somewhere. And we've already talked to Rusk." Frankly, based on his behavior the last time she had seen him, she was afraid of him. So she was going to put off a visit to him for as long as she could.

"He did it. Why even bother talking to anyone else?"

"He's a hothead, for sure. And it wouldn't surprise me one bit to hear he's the one who killed her. But..."

"But?" Ida Mae snapped her head around to stare at Henny. "You think he's innocent?"

"Not exactly. But he seemed genuinely upset and surprised by Leyla's death."

"Guilty conscience, if you ask me," Ida Mae muttered.

"Maybe. Or maybe someone else is the killer."

"Or he worked *with* someone else to kill her."

"That's entirely possible."

Ida Mae sighed and folded her hands over the purse in her lap. "Well, there's his loony girlfriend. She had been pretty mad at Leyla. It's possible she'd been willing to help her man kill off Leyla."

"I guess..." Henny pondered the idea of a couple bonded so tight they'd help each other murder someone. Like Bonnie and Clyde. "It's possible, I suppose. I think I need to hear from the Jake Arnold guy first."

Henny put the truck in gear and backed out of the driveway.

After a few moments, Ida Mae added, "And then there's the stolen jewels." She shook her head and looked out the passenger window as they sped down the road. "That does sound like Cash."

"Yup. He's always had sticky fingers."

"I think 'dishonest' is engraved on his DNA. Wasn't one of our grandpas like that? Maybe thievery is genetic."

Henny chuckled. "According to the stories Momma used to tell, Great-grandpa Robards was like that. His nickname was Pirate for a reason."

After a few moments of deep thought, Ida Mae said, "Do you think Cash really did steal the jewels?"

"Probably."

"But he was at the house with Leyla, Amber, and Luke. How do you think he was able to manage it?"

"The same way a weasel gets into the chicken coop. Through the tiniest opening, indiscernible to non-weasels."

They stopped at a light in front of the Plum Good Cafe. A familiar-looking girl came out of the cafe with a bag and a cup.

She had long black hair held off her pale face with a skull-dotted bandeau. Her arms were covered in tattoos.

Henny said, "Isn't that Marcia, Prettie's maid?"

"I think so."

"Hold on." Henny whipped the truck to the right, plowing up the hill.

Ida Mae grabbed the *Oh, Crap!* handle above the window. "Have you lost your mind? What are you doing?"

"I want to talk to her," Henny said, flying into the parking lot and landing in a spot near Marcia's car.

Marcia paused, staring at Henny and Ida Mae.

Henny threw the truck in park and rolled down her window. "Hey, you're Marcia, right?"

The girl squinted with suspicion. "Yeah? Who are you?"

Henny said to Ida Mae, "Hold on just a minute. I'll be right back."

To Marcia, she said, "Sorry. I should've identified myself. I'm Henny Wiley, Prettie and Leyla's friend."

The girl relaxed. "Oh. Okay." She sipped her drink. "What's up?"

"It was awful what happened to Leyla, huh?"

"Yeah. Total bummer. I like Prettie and Luke. I hope they're handling this okay."

Henny nodded. She hemmed. She wanted to ask this girl all the questions burning through her mind, but she also didn't want to be rude or put the girl on the spot, make her so uncomfortable that she wouldn't answer any questions.

The girl gaped at her as if to say *What's your deal, lady?* "Is there something I can help you with?"

"Look, I'm not very good at sugarcoating things, so I'm just going to shoot you straight, all right?"

"Oookaaay."

"I heard you were once an addict?"

Marcia screwed up her face, her cheeks pinking. "Yeah, and?"

"Are you still clean?"

"That's a really personal question." Marcia's defenses were rising and growing pricklier.

"Sorry, I don't mean to offend you. It's just that I've heard it's possible you might be back on drugs, and that's why Leyla's jewels are now missing."

Marcia gazed at her with a mixture of disbelief and disgust. Her dark eyes glittered from behind her thick black eyeliner. "Are you kidding me right now, lady?" She scoffed and spun to walk away toward a small red Ford Fiesta covered with bumper stickers on the back.

Henny chased after her. "Look, again, I'm not trying to offend you. Really. I'm just trying to help my friend and my brother. You see, people are trying to blame him for stealing the jewels, and I want to help clear his name and bring peace to Prettie's mind."

The girl stopped. "So you accuse me, instead? Typical. I'm never going to get out from under this cloud of suspicion because of my past. What's the point of getting clean if I'll never be trusted again?"

"Whoa, now. I didn't say any of that. Sure, it might take a while to earn trust back, but you will as long as you keep behaving in a way to deserve the trust. It's going to take time. And being clean is important for *you*. So you can be healthy and happy."

Marcia scoffed and opened her car door.

"Please don't leave. I only want to talk."

"I'm not leaving. Yet. I just want to put down my muffin and coffee." She ducked inside to put down her food. "But I hope this is a short convo because my coffee is, like, getting cold." She crossed her arms and huffed, leaning against her dusty car. "So you think I stole some jewels or something?"

"No. I don't. I heard from someone else that you might be involved. I wanted to ask what you know about it."

She narrowed her eyes and tipped her head. "If I did steal jewels in order to buy drugs or whatever, do you think I would, like, actually tell you?"

This "convo" was going downhill, fast. "Did you like Leyla? Did y'all have any problems or fights?"

"Nah. Her son is kind of a slob, but I get paid to be a maid, so it's not like I can complain about it. Job security, amiright? I never had a problem with her, though. She seemed nice enough. I guess. Not quite as nice as Prettie. Leyla had a bit of a superior attitude, like I was beneath her. Prettie treats me like a human, you know?"

"How did Leyla act superior to you?"

"Snapping her fingers at me. Calling me 'hey, girl,' and bossing me around some."

"That had to be annoying."

She nodded. "Oh, yeah. I used to get so mad about it..." She shook her head, then blew out a breath and set her jaw. "But after talking it through in my group, I have a better perspective on it now."

"Group?"

"Group therapy at the church. I went into it after I got out of rehab. It helps me cope with the things that pushed me toward drugs to begin with."

"Oh. So, would you say you were angry enough to get revenge on Leyla somehow?"

"Look, I wasn't a big fan of hers. But I'm not a killer, if that's what you're getting at. Even when I was strung out on, like, a bunch of drugs. If I wanted revenge on Leyla, I would've done something like slash her tires or wash her lipstick with her white laundry. Stuff like that. I wouldn't *kill* her."

"Or maybe you'd steal her jewelry?"

"Excuse me?"

"Maybe you wanted some new tattoos and needed a way to pay for them. Or maybe you fell back into drugs?"

"Judge much?" She snorted a laugh. "Um, first off, some of these were paid for by my parents for my birthday or Christmas." She pointed at random places on her arm. "Second, my new boyfriend is a tattoo artist. So he did many of these. For free. I don't need to steal some socialite's tacky jewelry to buy my tats. Tattoos which cover burn scars from a childhood accident, by the way. And…" She bobbed her head as she spoke. "For the record, because I don't need a bunch of nonsense gossip getting around, I'm *not* back on drugs."

"Do you know who would want Leyla dead?"

"Other than her jerk ex-husband? Nope. I can't imagine anyone else who would want her dead."

"I see." Henny couldn't think of anything else to ask. None of this made any sense. "Well, thanks for your time. I'm sorry to bother you."

Marcia opened her car door, then paused. "So, I'm curious, who told you I did it?"

"I don't know if I should tell you. I don't want to get her in trouble because she did say she wasn't certain about it. She was guessing."

"She?"

"I probably shouldn't say…"

"Look, it's not like I can do anything to this person, right? Because, if I did, I'd go to jail, and I already have a record, so they wouldn't go easy on me. And I'm not trying to deal with all that mess since I'm putting my life back together. Also, you would be a witness against me, right? Because of this whole conversation. So, it's not like I can get revenge. I'm not interested in revenge anyway. But I feel I have a right to know who's talking crap about me so I can better watch my back. Maybe they'll try something against me."

Henny thought about it. Marcia wasn't wrong. Amber wasn't the type to get revenge, anyway. She seemed too gentle. But Marcia did have a right to know who she could trust and who she couldn't. Henny hemmed. "You didn't hear it from me, but Amber, Luke's girlfriend, said you might've had something to do with it. But, to be fair, she also said my brother, Cash, might've been involved. Which is why I'm asking questions."

Her eyes transformed into black slits, and a dark energy infused the air around them. "Amber, huh?" she scoffed. "Not surprising."

"Why do you say so?"

"That girl is a piece of work." She shook her head.

Henny studied Marcia, puzzled. She wasn't sure how much she could believe. Amber seemed like a good, decent sort of person. "Is there bad blood between you and Amber?"

Marcia didn't answer. She slammed her car door and sped away, squealing her tires out of the parking lot.

Henny pursed her lips and watched Marcia's little red car fly off. Maybe she should've kept her mouth shut.

10

Henny pulled onto the road and headed toward Owensboro Avenue on the west side of town.

"What was that all about?" Ida Mae asked.

"I wanted to get a feel for the girl. I thought she
might've had something to do with the missing jewels; but after
talking to her, I'm not so sure."

"Oh, yeah?"

"When I told her about Amber saying Cash might be involved in Leyla's death and the missing jewels, Marcia said Amber was a piece of work."

"Huh. Interesting."

"Then, when I asked her if there was bad blood between them,
she wouldn't say anything. She jumped in her car and drove off."

"Weird."

"I thought so."

"Maybe we need to talk to her again," Ida Mae suggested.

A comfortable silence settled between them as they passed
through the historic town of Plumridge, past the rowhouses dating back to the mid-1800s that had long since been converted
into businesses. Each building in the row was painted a different
color: pink, aqua, olive green, yellow, blue, red, and black, like
brick crayons encircling the red brick Federalist style courthouse
at the center.

They took the first road on the right off the town square and headed down a neatly landscaped and shady street lined with poplar trees and pristine Victorian and Edwardian homes. It was as though time had been frozen and Henny and Ida Mae had entered a portal to a distant era. Henny almost expected to see horses and buggies and women in hoop skirts and men in tall hats populating the streets. But she saw only shiny high-end cars, jogging women in yoga pants, and men in shorts carrying golf clubs.

They passed out of the neighborhood into a developed area full of shops, banks, boutiques, a plaza, and a convenience store. A large, brown-brick modern building with beige cornices sat on the right side of Owensboro Avenue. Henny parked in the visitor parking in front of the building.

She and Ida Mae entered the glass door, passed the plants, wall fountains, and the sleek modernist lobby full of black-leather furniture and glass tables. They approached the reception desk at the back of the building, where a pretty, athletic woman in a tight red sweater sat under the gold letters reading Altamonte Realty against a wall of gray marble tile.

"I'm here to see Jake Arnold," Henny said.

"Do you have an appointment?"

"No. I, uh, am new in the market and I was referred to him by a friend."

The woman pasted a saccharine smile on her face. "Please have a seat in the lobby, and I'll see if Jake is available to speak with you."

The amount of fake sweetness oozing from the woman made Henny's teeth hurt.

She and Ida Mae sat in the lobby and flipped through dream home magazines.

After about ten minutes, a man in his thirties approached. He had short dark hair and a stubbled jawline. His black golf shirt revealed tan, toned arms. He was a fit man who enjoyed outdoor activity, and his quick step and squared shoulders indicated a confidence bordering on cockiness, quick energy, and most likely a quick temper to match. He pointed at the receptionist. "Hey there, sweetheart. Looking good today."

The receptionist smiled tightly, then rolled her eyes behind his back.

"Hey, there." Jake smiled, shoving his hand at Henny and Ida Mae for a strong shake that made Henny's hand ache. The corners of his hazel eyes pleated. "I'm Jake. I heard you ladies were looking for me. How can I help you? Are you in the market to buy, or sell?"

"Neither," Henny said. "I'm here to ask you just a couple of questions, if you don't mind."

His smile faded. "About what?" His hawkish eyes darted between the women, lighting with suspicion.

"We're friends of Leyla Hager. You worked with her, right?"

"Yeah, uh..." He planted his hands on his hips. "I heard about what happened to her when the cops came out here asking questions. But I didn't know anything to tell them. We didn't always get along, but I'm really sorry about what happened to her. Is there anything I can do to help the family or..." He let his voice trail off.

"No. I don't think so. We had heard there was a big blowout between you two," Henny said.

"Hm. You can't always believe rumors." He put on his most charming smile. He glanced around and rubbed his beak nose.

"Leyla's sister isn't exactly the rumor mill, though," Ida Mae said, crossing her arms over her generous bosom.

"I don't know what Leyla told her sister, but I'm sure it wasn't the truth."

"What makes you say so?" Henny asked.

"I don't know. Leyla had a way of embellishing things."

"You're saying she's a liar?"

He pinned Henny with a hard stare. "Not necessarily. I don't know what she said to her sister, but I assume if you're here asking me questions about it, it couldn't have been good."

"What would Leyla have to gain from lying to her sister about you?"

Jake shrugged and checked his Apple watch, poking the screen. "Maybe her sister is just...confused."

"Can you at least tell us what the dustup was about?"

"Why? You're not the police. I don't have to talk to you."

"No, you don't," Henny said. "But I was hoping you would talk to us out of the kindness of your heart. To help give closure to her sister and son."

He nodded. "Look..." He pulled his phone out of his pocket and texted as he spoke. "I promise you I've cooperated fully with the police. Told them everything I know. I'm truly sorry for your loss. I wish I could talk longer, but I have an appointment." He tapped the earbud in his ear. "Hey, man. Sure. No, I'm on my way. One sec." He spoke to Henny and Ida Mae. "Thanks for coming out, ladies, but I have work to do. If you're ever in the market to buy or sell, let me know. Evie, over there"—he pointed to the receptionist—"has a business card for you. Have a good day. Again, really sorry about Leyla." He strode away, talking to whoever was in his ear. He patted Evie's desk as he passed it.

She pinched off a smile with barely a glance in his direction. Henny's brows lifted. Evie didn't seem to think much of Jake.

Ida Mae said, "Well, that was a waste of time."

"Maybe not."

"Why do you say so?"

Henny whispered to Ida Mae, "I get the impression Evie doesn't like him much and might be willing to talk."

The sisters smiled at each other.

"Hey, there," Henny said. "Evie, is it?"

"Yes. How can I help you?" the polished blonde said.

"I need to get one of Jake's business cards."

Evie went through the cards on her desk and handed one to Henny.

Henny tucked the card in her purse as she spoke. "So, Jake is something else, huh?"

Evie chuckled. "Sure is."

Henny sensed the tension between the girl's dislike of Jake and her desire to remain professional.

Ida Mae said, "You know, you look familiar. What's your last name?"

"Grayson."

"Evie Grayson," Ida Mae muttered. "Grayson, Grayson."

Henny watched Ida Mae's mind click through five decades of names and faces from Plumridge. Between the two of them, they knew a large portion of the town. And it was always easier to extract information from an acquaintance than from a stranger.

Ida Mae brightened. "Wait a minute! Are you Lonnie Grayson's granddaughter?"

"Yes, ma'am."

"He and I go way back. He asked me out to our homecoming dance in high school and we had the best time. He sure could dance back in the day too. But then he went into the Marines and we went our separate ways. I always thought highly of him."

Evie brightened. "My grandpa dancing?" She stifled a laugh. "It's hard to imagine him dancing, since he putters around with a walker now."

"Aw," Henny said. "That's a shame. Was he injured?"

"He had a stroke a few years ago and he never really has recovered."

"I'm sorry to hear it," Ida Mae said. "He whipped me around the floor like a carnival ride."

Evie giggled. "What's your name? I'll tell him I met you."

"I'm Ida Mae Puckett. Back then, Ida Mae Cooper. And this here's my sister, Henny Wiley."

"Oh," Evie said. "How cool. So nice to meet y'all."

"Yeah." Ida Mae nodded. "I've kept up with y'all's family through the years. I remember when you were born. Back then your family was going to our church and I remember the little Christmas play all y'all kids put on. You played baby Jesus because you were the only newborn in the congregation that year."

Evie tipped her head. "I don't remember that, of course, but my mom told me about it. Apparently, I threw up on one of the Wise Men."

Ida Mae laughed. "Oh, yes. We were tickled about it for days after. You made quite an impression on everyone."

They all laughed. Henny laughed with them, despite not being able to remember this girl, her family, or the Christmas play, even though she'd been there. When the laughter faded, and Henny believed Evie was warmed up to talk, she jumped in. "Fun times." She paused. "So, Evie, maybe you could help us." Henny leaned on the countertop and lowered her voice. "You knew Leyla Hager, right?"

"Oh, yes," Evie said, her face marked with pity. "I hated to hear about her death. Do y'all know the funeral arrangements yet? I'd like to go to the viewing at least. Maybe send some flowers. She was always so nice to me."

"Thank you, that's really sweet of you," Henny said. "We don't know any of the details yet. I think the body is still with the medical examiner. You know, because of the investigation."

Evie's face twisted with sympathy. "So sad. How're Prettie and Luke handling it?"

"As good as could be expected, I guess."

Ida Mae said, "How long has Jake worked here?"

Henny flashed a knowing glance at her sister, thankful that she'd turned the conversation back to a spot for convenient nosing around.

Evie said, "About five years or so."

"Is he popular?" Ida Mae asked.

"Meh." Evie shrugged.

That was the signal Henny needed. "He seems...difficult to get along with."

Evie made a face. "That's putting it nicely." She flushed to the roots of her blond hair and she whispered, "Gosh. I'm so sorry. That wasn't very professional of me."

Henny smiled. "No worries, sweetie. We ain't going to tell anyone. You're young, you're pretty. I'm sure he has behaved unprofessionally toward you a time or two."

Evie glanced around and lowered her voice. "He makes me uncomfortable."

Henny's brows shot up. "Is he hitting on you? If he is, you need to report him."

"There's some of that, but I just ignore it. The biggest issue..." she whispered, "he loses his temper really easily and he says mean things."

"Why does the company keep him?"

"He's the top salesman. A cash cow. So, basically, he gets to do what he wants. But I'm looking for other work, so I won't have to put up with him much longer."

Henny turned this information over in her mind. A cocky man with a short temper. Maybe Leyla pushed his buttons and ended up dead. "I just have to ask..." Henny said. "And I understand if you can't tell me. Do you know if he and Leyla had any kind of blowout? I heard there was some friction between them."

Evie hemmed. "I really shouldn't—"

"Look, I get it. You don't want to get in trouble. But you just said you were looking to get out of here anyway. And it would bring an enormous amount of peace to Prettie and Luke if you shared what you know."

"Are you working with the police?"

"Not directly..." Henny said. "I'm trying to find out some information on my own, because I don't want my innocent brother implicated in something he didn't do."

"Well..." Evie paused, thinking. She sighed. "They did fight. It was after the building was shut down for the night. I had gone upstairs to collect my things. Everyone else was gone and, at first, they didn't know I was upstairs. I was in the break room, but I could hear them shouting all the way down the hall."

"What were they shouting about?" Henny and Ida Mae said in unison.

She held up her hands. "I don't pretend to understand all of it. But it was about some kind of shady dealings. Apparently, she had caught him selling houses with hidden damage or something to people."

Henny pushed up her glasses. "I don't understand. Don't they hire an inspector to find the damage?"

"Yeah, he and an inspector were working together. The inspector didn't report the damage so Jake could make the sale on a lemon. Leyla was screaming about reporting him. And he screamed back that he would, in his words, 'destroy her.' It chilled my blood." She shuddered and hugged herself, rubbing her upper arms. "Then as I was coming out of the break room, they came out of his office and saw me. They stopped arguing and I rushed out. The look on his face scared me. All wild and crazy. The next day, Jake came up to me and told me I should forget about everything I had just heard." Her voice shook. "Then he grew really calm and scary-like and said, 'I'd hate for anything to happen to you.' Then he touched my cheek." She blew out a nervous breath. "Creeped me out."

"Wow," Ida Mae said. "So scary."

Evie nodded, terror flashing in her eyes.

"When did this happen?"

"Last week."

"Did you try to contact the managers here about the fraud or the police about the threats?"

"Lord, no! I'm not stupid. He knows where I work. And where I live. He knows I live alone." Tears filled her eyes. "I'm too afraid to even walk out to my car by myself. I always go with someone now."

"Do you think he might try to hurt you?" Ida Mae asked.

"I don't know. And I'm not going to trust him enough to find out."

Henny said, "If you're that scared, though, why are you telling us?"

"I feel a little better knowing that someone else knows. In case something happens to me."

"You should go to the police."

Evie shook her head. "Nope. I've seen *Lifetime* movies. I know how this story goes. I say something to alert the police, they question him but don't arrest him because they need time to investigate or don't have enough evidence. Then he comes after me in the meantime. I get a protective order, which does nothing, and I end up at the bottom of a lake in the next county. I've written anonymous letters to the managers and the police, which I will have delivered to them by a friend after I've gotten a new job and a new home."

"It's a small town, Evie..." Henny said. "He'll find you."

She scoffed. "I'm not staying here. I'm looking for a place out of state, closer to my parents. They moved recently for their retirement. No one here knows that. Then I'm going to completely ghost this place. I've already shut down all my social media and changed my phone number. I'm not hanging around."

This poor girl reminded her of her late friend Jenna Lawson. Young, pretty, blonde, terrified. Henny said a silent prayer for this girl's safety. "I'm so sorry you're going through this, hon. You stay safe, okay?"

Evie nodded, biting her lower lip and offering a timid smile.

Ida Mae checked her phone and said, "We've taken enough of your time. Thank you for helping us."

Henny's heart twisted for Evie. "When you're ready to leave, you let me know and I'll deliver the letters."

"Oh, you don't have to do that."

"Nope. I will. Here's my address." Henny pulled a sheet of paper out of her purse and wrote down her address. "You send them to me, then I'll personally take them to the proper people. I want to see the jerk in jail so you don't have to keep looking over your shoulder."

"That's so kind of you. Maybe I will."

They said their goodbyes, and Henny and Ida Mae returned to the truck.

"Poor girl," Henny said.

"I know. I hope she's able to escape to safety." Ida Mae dug in her purse. "She's in a horrible predicament." She pulled out a tube of hand lotion and put a dab in her hands. "I can understand why she was terrified, though. It's too hard to get real protection in these 'she said, he said' type cases." She rubbed the lotion into her hands.

"It is. But she gave us some important information. Seems Jake might be a dangerous hothead."

"Seems so. He certainly had the motive."

"Maybe we've found Leyla's killer."

Henny and Ida Mae crossed town to the north side where the more modern, middle-class homes stood, packed like sardines on neatly trimmed lawns. They wove through the maze of subdivision streets, ending up at Bellevue Avenue.

After a few minutes of searching, Ida Mae said, "There's Susan's house!" She tapped the window with her finger.

"Stop touching the window," Henny said. "You're leaving greasy fingerprints all over the glass."

"Are you kidding me right now?" Ida Mae gaped at her. "There's at least six inches of dust and dirt all over your truck and you're concerned about my fingerprints on the window?"

"You're leaving smudges everywhere, though, and I have to see out the windows. I don't need to see out the sides of my truck."

"Oh, for Pete's sake," Ida Mae groused, pulling the sleeve of her sweatshirt over her hand and wiping the smudges off the glass. "What is wrong with you? Is your blood sugar low or something?"

With a huff, Henny threw the truck into park behind a blue car and a silver car. The sisters marched up the drive to the front door. The house had large beams of wood supporting the porch roof and a porch swing. Except for the overgrown shrubs and unraked leaves in the front yard, the house looked like something Chip and Joanna Gaines from *Fixer Upper* might've built—modern with a rustic flair.

Ida Mae was about to speak, but Henny put her finger to her mouth. "Listen," she whispered. They stood still, ears trained on the two female voices coming from within. Sounded like an argument.

After listening for a few moments, Ida Mae whispered, "I can't make out what they're saying."

"Me either, but it sounds pretty heated." Henny jabbed the doorbell.

The voices stopped and the door jerked open. A scowling Susan stood there in a white tank top, covered with a large gray sweater, and blue lounge pants, her dark greasy hair pulled back in a messy bun. One hand held a wine glass, half-full.

Henny raised her brows. Kind of early in the day for wine. *But to each her own, I suppose.*

"Can I help you?" Her tone indicated that helping someone was the very last thing on her mind. Henny was glad she didn't need any real help.

"Uh, Susan Elsher?"

"Yes?"

"My name is Henny Wiley, and this is my sister Ida Mae. We're friends of Prettie Davis."

Susan sipped her wine, leaned against the doorjamb, and continued to etch disdain into her features. "Okay."

Henny's attention was caught by a young woman moving in the background. She had dark, slick-straight hair. She grabbed a purple and silver cheerleader uniform from a nearby peg. The girl made a face at Susan's back and marched from the room in a huff. Susan pushed her chin forward as if to say *Spit it out, idiot.*

"Uhm, I was there the day you and Leyla had an...interaction. And since then, she's been murdered."

Henny didn't think it was possible for the lines around Susan's mouth to get any deeper. But now they ran deep enough to give her the appearance of a marionette. "I heard. I'm real sorry about it. I didn't like her, but she didn't deserve to die, I guess."

"May I ask why you didn't like her?"

She raked her dark, bleary eyes over Henny. Her words slurred a little. "Because she was a witch who stuck her nose where it didn't belong. And when I tried to tell her once to back off, she wouldn't listen. So I caught her out at Prettie's. Now my daughter has all kinds of ridiculous ideas bouncing around in her head. I don't like speaking ill of the dead, but..." She shook her head and drank a sip of wine. "Anyway, so what does this have to do with anything?"

Henny didn't want to come right out and accuse this woman. Mostly because she wasn't sure she could take her if Susan decided to get physical. She looked pretty fit. And mean. Like Henny's daddy always said, *It ain't the size of the dog in the fight. It's the size of the fight in the dog.* Which was true to a point, she supposed. Henny didn't want to find out. Besides, just because Susan and

Leyla had disagreements didn't mean Susan had killed her, and it was pretty ugly to accuse an innocent woman of murder.

Susan's impatient sigh snapped Henny out of her reverie. "Oh, uh, my brother Cash was with Leyla that day. And the police seem to be interested in him. I'm talking to everyone I can to see if there might be someone else who might've wanted to hurt her." Even though she wanted to wring her brother's neck right now and she wanted to see him move from her house, she preferred that he move to an apartment rather than a jail cell.

Susan narrowed her eyes. "Are you accusing me of something, lady?"

Her instant aggression caught Henny off-guard. "Oh, uh, I-I-uh..."

"Hold on." Susan lifted her hand to stop her. "Look, let me keep it real simple for y'all." She lowered her hand to plant it on her hip. "I didn't like Leyla. She was always getting between Rusk and me. And my daughter, Jill. When she started putting fool ideas in my daughter's head about joining the cheerleading squad when I explicitly told Jill she couldn't..." Her head bobbed on her neck and she used her wine glass hand to emphasize her words, the dark liquid sloshing erratically with her movements. "That's when I stepped in and put her in her place. Did I confront her over at Prettie's? Yes, ma'am, I did, and I'd do it again. She's lucky I didn't run her over with my car. But did I *kill* her? No." She stood straight. "And *you* ought to be embarrassed, coming out here to my house to ask me if I'm a killer. You hear me?" She stepped out on the porch, forcing Henny to take a step back. Clearly, this woman was just looking for a reason to throw hands.

Irritation crept over the back of Henny's neck. Her first instinct was to step forward and stand toe to toe, but de-escalation was the smarter, classier thing to do. Even though her hand tingled to slap Susan's sassy mouth. So, Henny stepped back and lifted her hands in surrender. "I'm not trying to accuse you of anything."

Ida Mae wedged herself between the women. "You really need to calm down. No one is trying to start a fight here."

"We're only trying to clear our brother's name," Henny added. "I don't want him in trouble for something he didn't do."

"Fine. But you need to hunt somewhere else, because I didn't do anything she didn't deserve. Now, are we done?"

"Yep. I'm done."

Ida Mae nudged her toward the porch steps. "C'mon. Let's go."

Susan's daughter, Jill, pushed past her mother. "I'm late for work." She was a pretty girl, dressed in a short purple peasant dress revealing long, lean, spray-tanned legs. Her slick, dark hair fell down her back and her brown almond-shaped eyes were framed with the thick eyebrows popular among the young girls at the moment.

"Where are you going in those boots?" Susan asked.

They all looked down at the black Doc Marten combat-style boots.

"Work," Jill answered with a sixteen-year-old attitude.

"Your boss lets you wear those? They don't seem very professional."

The girl huffed. "They're fine, Mom. Gosh, relax. Have another glass of wine." She spun with attitude.

"Hey," Susan shouted at her back. "A little respect. I wouldn't have to drink if you acted better."

Henny and Ida Mae exchanged a wide-eyed gaze.

"Whatever," she shouted. Jill jumped in her little blue Chevy Sonic and peeled out of the drive, a big yellow daisy sticker on the bumper disappearing down the road.

Susan slid her bleary eyes over to Henny and Ida Mae. "You have something you want to say?"

Henny shook her head slowly. "Nope. I think I'm done."

"Good." Susan turned and stepped back into her house. "Don't come back." She slammed the door and locked it.

"Nasty ol' woman," Ida Mae said as they turned back to the truck.

"You got that right," Henny added. "Lord help her daughter. Must be awful to have a mother like that."

11

After Henny dropped Ida Mae off at The Shack to pick up her car, she turned her truck toward home. It had been a long day. The sun was now sinking toward the horizon, leaving a play of amber light and shadow across the yards and buildings she passed.

Once home, she had the house to herself. Both Cash and Walter were absent, and a mixture of loneliness and relief settled around her like blackberry brambles. She thought a hot supper of vegetable soup and a grilled-cheese sandwich would calm her, but it didn't. She couldn't stop thinking about Rusk, Susan, Marcia, Amber, Jake, and Cash. So many people and no clear suspect. Which meant also no clear path to justice for Prettie or Henny's own family. She tried to crochet her anxiety into a coherent shape, but that, too, failed her. In fact, it only aggravated her, because she kept getting her yarn in knots and messing up the pattern. She finally threw it aside in frustration.

A frustration that spread throughout her body like itchy wool—an old familiar feeling with only one cure. She tried to fight it, to distract herself because she knew digging for treasure would only get her in trouble. But the more she fought it, the stronger and deeper the sensation grew. She rose from her chair, stuffed her feet into her gardening boots, and grabbed her jacket, purse, and keys. She wasn't at all happy about it, either. Henny felt as though she were being pulled through the motions by an external force rather than moving of her own volition. For the first time, she wasn't excited about the treasures or about diving.

Henny visited the Ladybug Consignment first. She thought about avoiding this location because of what had happened here a few weeks ago. In fact, she'd considered not going at all, but it was impossible to change the routine. It was too unsettling, as though something was out of place, not right, like a half-painted wall or a half-decorated Christmas tree. It would throw her completely out of balance to disrupt her habits.

She sat in her truck gazing at the dumpster. Apprehension stabbed at her. She hadn't been here since...she swallowed the hard lump in her throat. Jenna. She'd found Jenna's body here. The dumpster glowed in her headlights. Maybe she should go back home. Or to another dumpster.

Henny blew out a breath. She wanted to go, but her compulsions drove her forward anyway. The Thing inside her, whatever it was, wouldn't let her turn away. She slid from the truck and moved around to the bed, where she removed her diving kit: a white metal stepladder tied to a blue milk crate with a yellow boat-line; and a sparkly pink messenger bag, which she hung diagonally over her body. Removing the headlamp from the messenger bag, she turned it on and pulled it down over her unruly hair. She approached her target, opened the stepladder, climbed up, and pushed open the dumpster's side door with some effort. Lowering the milk crate into the dumpster, she scanned the interior for dangerous objects and startled critters.

The bundles inside the metal container sang out to her, luring her, drawing her in. She sat on the edge of the opening, her feet dangling inside the dumpster, the metal digging uncomfortably into her rear. Maybe just one more dive. A tension rose in her chest and arms. Then she could maybe taper off and find some other way to fight against the Thing in these moments. But what? Nothing soothed her and made her feel whole like finding a precious treasure, carrying it home, and giving it a special place in her house.

She jumped down into the dumpster, landing on a pile of large chunks of Styrofoam, and lost herself in opening bags and digging through piles. Ultimately, she found a bookend shaped like a cherub. Not the most fruitful dive, but it was something. Henny climbed out of the dumpster, gathered her things, and moved on to her next favorite spot behind the beauty salon. She had found some good-smelling peach shampoo and conditioner there a couple of months ago. The large pump bottle had still been half-full! The same excitement and joy from the first time she'd smelled that fresh peach scent pressed through the displeasure, easing her mind into a peaceful numbness as she beelined to the Luxe Locks Salon in the Plumridge Plaza on Franklin Avenue.

Diving at this salon made her feel less like a cheater. After all, she and her sister Ida Mae had frequented Sassy Styles for years. So she didn't feel right about going through their dumpster. Thinking of Sassy's made her shiver. The last time she'd been there, she'd been involved in a fight with some bad guys. But Luxe Locks was the competition. One of those youthful, flashy salons with the loud music and bright colors, catering to all the latest trends. It was the place where most of the young people, and older women fighting age like a menopausal honey badger, frequented.

Once again, she pulled out her diving kit, climbed inside the dumpster, and rummaged through the refuse, squeezing the bags to discern whether they contained actual garbage or treasures. After all, Henny had no use for half-eaten food, empty cups, used tissues, or other gross things. Finally, at the bottom she found a bag full of hard items in small round and tall cylindrical shapes. Excitement fizzled in her fingertips, and she eagerly tore the bag open like a raccoon falling upon a bag of french fries.

She gazed upon the bottles of shampoo, conditioner, texture spray, modeling gel, and other cosmetics. Whatever misgivings she'd started with soon dissipated as she opened each bottle to take in their fragrances. She cast aside the ones scented like herbs or the bitter odor of marigolds. Finally, Henny found one scented like tangy green apples and another with a calming lavender perfume. She also found some aromatherapy oils: orange blossom, vanilla, and jasmine. She tucked all these treasures into her glittery messenger bag.

Something shiny caught her eyes. She bent down and retrieved a clear acrylic box full of teeny rhinestones and sparkling baubles of various shapes, like the little doodads women put on their nails. Near this lay a few bottles of dried-up nail polish: purple, pink, baby blue, and red. Among these, she noticed a small silver star. She'd seen that star before. It looked like the star on the glittery purple fingernail she'd found the night she discovered Leyla's body.

Henny dug in her messenger bag and found the nail to compare the stars. It was, in fact, the same star. So maybe this nail came from this salon. She looked at the back of the brick building, lit with a security light. A stray cat trotted past the door. But, it was possible that the star on this nail had come from any of the salons in town. It probably meant nothing.

She dropped everything into her bag, then dove in one more time. When her hands fell on something pliable, Henny pulled, broke the surface of the bags and boxes, and held it up like a fisherman with his prize trout. A purse. Like a white crescent moon.

Henny's mouth dropped open. "Oh, my stars! This looks just like Leyla's purse."

She studied the little leather purse with its gold links attaching the strap. There was blood splattered on it, and a smudge of blood around the corner where the zipper head rested. Inside, she found gum, lipstick, a wadded tissue, a small vial of perfume, and a compact mirror. No wallet. It couldn't have fallen out into the dumpster, because the purse was closed when she found it. Likely whoever killed her had dumped the purse here—after stealing her wallet, which likely had credit cards, cash, checkbook, identification, and any number of items to steal. "I wonder how much money she was carrying," Henny muttered to herself.

She needed to take this to the sheriff. Now.

The sheriff wasn't at the station: Henny spoke with a short, stout female deputy named McNally.

Henny looked her over. "You must be a new recruit. I've never seen you before."

The woman's voice was deep and raspy. "I am. I started last week."

"Are you sure you know what you're doing?"

McNally's thin auburn brows arched, and irritation flashed in her dull green eyes. "I graduated at the top of my class, ma'am. I think I'm more than equipped to take something into evidence."

Henny flushed. "I'm sorry, hon. I don't mean to offend you. It's just that the lady who owned this purse was killed recently. I'm a friend of the family. It's important for things to be done properly so whoever did this can get caught and rot in jail."

McNally softened some, but an air of indignance settled around her. "What did you find?"

Henny held out a plastic shopping bag. "This purse. It belonged to Leyla Hager."

McNally opened the bag and peered inside. "Looks like there's blood on it."

"That's what I thought too."

She lowered the bag and pinned Henny with an analytical stare. "Where did you find this?"

Uh-oh. Now this was a pickle. She couldn't lie, because the police would likely want to go back to the dumpster to look for more evidence. Which would be a good thing if they found something to help the case. But if Henny told her the truth, McNally might think she was a complete loon. After all, normal people didn't dig around in dumpsters. *But wait. I'm normal,* Henny thought. *Right?* Maybe. She slammed the door on that thought. She found treasures. She liked treasure-hunting. But she had to tell something to this McNally woman who was beginning to narrow her eyes and tip her head in suspicion. "Well, I...uh...I came across it behind the Luxe Locks Salon."

"Okay. Where?"

Henny's face burned hot. "In the dumpster," she muttered.

"Did you say *in* the dumpster?"

"Yes." Her mind wheeled, clicking her story into place as she spoke. "I had some garbage in my truck and I decided to throw it away in the dumpster. I just happened to see the purse in there. At first I was going to ignore it, but then when I saw the blood I thought I should bring it to y'all."

"You know it's illegal to dump your trash in a dumpster a company is paying for."

Fear shot through Henny. She didn't want to have to pay a

fine for something she hadn't actually done. "It wasn't a bunch of trash. Just one bag the size of that shopping bag." Defensiveness scratched behind her chest. "Besides, I figured you'd be more concerned about the bloody purse, which could be key evidence in the recent murder case. I guess I could've ignored it and left it there. That should be worth something, don't you think?" She shifted side to side and looked at their reflection in the exit door.

McNally pinched her lips together, thinking. Then she nodded. "Right. Look, I won't fine you this time. But don't do it again."

"I won't."

"Did you see anyone or anything in the vicinity that seemed out of place or unusual?"

"No."

"Did you happen to recover her phone?"

"No."

"Hm. It wasn't near the body when it was recovered. Maybe it fell down into the dumpster. I'll get another deputy and we'll go out there to search for it."

"Well, you can search if you like, but that purse was closed when I found it. I guess it's possible the phone was thrown in separately."

McNally nodded. "Right. Okay. I'll go look anyway. Just in case. I'll put this into evidence, and we'll check the business cameras. But it's likely the sheriff will have more questions for you."

They said their goodbyes, and McNally returned to the interior of the station while Henny made a dash for her truck. The temperature had dropped, and the icy wind cut like razors against her skin. She buzzed all over with fear, irritation, and anxiety as though she'd downed too much caffeine.

Henny jammed her key into the ignition and watched the moths fluttering around the security light at the station. Then she noticed movement at the front of the building. A young girl exited the building in a cheerleader outfit. She wore a purple jacket and purple sweatpants under her skirt to protect against the cold. Her face was lit up in the light from her phone as she texted and walked toward her car.

Henny rolled down her window. "Amber?"

Amber stopped and looked at her. "Yes?"

"Henny Wiley. We met at Prettie's."

"Oh, yeah. Hey, Mrs. Wiley."

"What are you doing out here?"

Amber walked toward her truck. Silver glitter covered her heavily made-up face and sparkled in her hair, which was pulled into a ponytail ornamented with purple and silver ribbons. Her sickly sweet perfume like cotton candy and vanilla tickled Henny's nose. "I had to give a statement about Leyla. You know, since I was one of the last to see her."

"I see. How long were you in there?"

"Maybe an hour. Had to write out a statement." She smacked her gum and blew a bubble.

"So they didn't interrogate you?"

"Not really." She continued to text. "They asked a few questions, then asked me to write out everything."

"What'd you tell them?"

Amber said, "The same thing I told you at Prettie's the other day." Her thumbs flew over the letters on the screen as she spoke. Henny noticed her nails: purple glitter with silver stars. Like the one she'd found at the crime scene. Henny studied Amber, then craned her neck to try to see what she was typing. Amber continued, "I didn't have my car, so Leyla took me and Cash to my brother's house."

Henny blinked rapidly and froze.

Amber glanced up, caught the look on Henny's face. A dark glimmer entered her eyes as she tucked the phone in her jacket pocket. "I gotta go. I'm cheering at the football game tonight." A crooked smile crossed her face, and a hollowness entered her voice. "You take care."

She spun around and jogged away, ponytail swinging.

A chill trickled over Henny. The girl had just lied to her.

12

enny pondered her conversation with Amber as she drove from the sheriff's station. She turned right onto an old country road stripped of the artificial glow of street lights and business signs, guided only by the dim headlights of her white Ford pickup. Maybe Amber hadn't actually *lied*. Maybe she'd misremembered something or messed up her words. After all, she had been texting while speaking. Henny couldn't completely discount Amber, she supposed. Even though she was just a girl, a respectful, polite young lady. Amber might've been was among the last to see Leyla alive, but she couldn't believe for a minute that Amber would be so vicious or evil.

Her mind turned to Leyla and flashes of her poor, crumpled body in the burned-out car. Then rose the grieved faces of Prettie and Luke who were racked with sorrow over the loss of their sister, mother, and friend. Yet so little seemed to be known about Leyla's death. She had been murdered. That much was clear. Her ex, Ruskin, seemed unhinged with jealousy and a visceral, unfocused rage at anything and everything.

Henny knew she'd been murdered. She knew the murderer had taken her purse from the kill site to throw it in the dumpster. Or, perhaps, Leyla was killed somewhere else and the killer thought to distract the police by dumping the purse in a completely random spot. Further, the police hadn't yet located her cell phone. It could be anywhere. But why was she killed? The missing jewelry seemed as likely a motive as any. But who would want the jewelry? And why? Surely Ruskin wouldn't want them. Unless he was in severe money problems—and, according to Prettie, it did seem like he was struggling financially. And if Leyla stood to ruin him in the divorce, it would make sense that he might want her dead. Yet, beneath the surface of his anger, he'd seemed genuinely concerned about Leyla. Was he that good an actor? Henny supposed it was possible.

Then there was Ruskin's girlfriend, Susan. She didn't like Leyla. She'd assaulted her and threatened her. Susan did say she would "end" Leyla if she talked to her daughter again. Maybe Leyla talked to the girl and riled up Susan's anger. But then would Susan have access to the jewels? It was entirely possible that the missing jewels weren't related to the murder.

Then there was the maid at Prettie's house on the day of the murder. She wasn't the most likely suspect for the murder, but she might've stolen the jewelry. It was also entirely possible that one person killed Leyla for one reason and someone else stole the jewels for reasons entirely unconnected to the murder.

And the realtor, Jake Arnold. Hothead. Stalker. Cocky. And doing shady things, cheating people into buying damaged homes by having his buddy inspector sign off on the inspection reports. Leyla had caught him. They'd fought. Maybe he saw her while she was out dropping off Amber and Cash, and Jake followed her. Then when he discovered her alone, he attacked her, dumped her body in an isolated area, and set the car on fire to destroy evidence.

Then there was Cash. He drove Henny crazy and got under her skin like scabies mites. No denying that. But she knew he was no murderer. Cash had a soft heart, despite his questionable morality and behavior. Though Ida Mae, Walter, and her own better judgment had warned Henny against taking him into her home, she couldn't help it. She would always think of him as her baby brother. The little guy who wore feet pajamas, played with G.I. Joe, and slept with a nightlight and a ratty teddy bear until almost twelve years old. She still remembered the sweet boy who loved to draw, read comic books, and communed with nature while enduring the scathing remarks and blows of bullies at school, targeting a frail-looking boy easily broken and cowed into submission. Every day he came home with a new black eye, new bruises on his face. She often heard him crying in his room. Even now it wrung her heart and tears stung her eyes to think of the sweet boy he'd once been. Sure, he'd pestered and picked on her until she flew into a rage, but she still loved him and carried a soft spot in her heart for him.

But when Cash hit sixteen, he'd changed. Started hanging out with a rough, ragtag crowd of boys who gave trouble a new meaning. Drinking, drugs, stealing, fighting, vandalism, and every other horrible thing they could contrive to terrorize the community. He started going to jail and making Momma and Daddy cry, and Henny's heart had begun to harden toward him. For a long time, she'd tried to cover for Cash, to help him shelter their parents from the trouble he was causing and living in. Their parents had always believed Cash would eventually grow out of it, and Henny and Ida Mae had hoped they were right. Henny kept hoping Cash would come home one day to announce that he was turning his life around. But he never did. And now, maybe he was beyond help. She sighed and sank into herself.

The grass on the side of the road looked like little skeletons, and the occasional eyes of critters blinked out of the darkness. She slowed her speed. It was November. Deer season. There would be scores of them on these dark country roads. As if the thought had pulled the animal out of thin air, a large buck with at least a ten-point rack stood in the middle of the road and stared her down, challenging her to a duel. She honked her horn until he loped away.

"Stupid buck."

Though Cash had never turned his life around to walk the straight-and-narrow, he was not the stuff of a murderer, even if he had stolen the jewels. There were other people who were more likely the murderer.

Henny pulled up into her driveway and dragged herself to the screened porch. All she wanted was to slip into her pajamas and bunny slippers and curl up with a cup of hot cocoa and some TV. No murder shows tonight. Tonight she wanted to watch *Everybody Loves Raymond* or some other comedy.

She put the key in the lock and turned it. When she opened the door, she heard a thump and some hectic whispers. She perked up. "Walter? Is that you?"

"Gogogogo," a male voice hissed, followed by a series of thumps and rumblings as the guy or guys, no doubt, tripped over the boxes and containers and magazines.

"Who's there?" She flipped on the lights in the kitchen in time to catch a black tennis shoe disappearing into the living room. "Oh, my Lord!" she shouted. She dropped her stuff on the floor and rushed to the landline phone. Well, tried to, but the piles of treasures made it difficult to rush anywhere. She grabbed the phone and headed toward the living room. The door stood open, and voices echoed in the darkness.

Henny quickly sidestepped around the fallen boxes. She flipped on the porch light, but saw only shadows slipping into more shadows. Then she heard car doors slam and the squeal of tires. She stepped onto the porch and craned her neck to try to see the car, but could see only the glare of red taillights.

Henny called the police to report the intrusion. Deputy McNally arrived bundled up in her uniform coat and hat. Henny allowed her entrance to the home and said, "When I came home there was at least two people in here. I heard them talking, then they rushed out my front door."

McNally looked around the room, her gaze tripping over boxes, bags, containers, and papers and such. "Did you see the intruders or how they got away?"

"No. They were too fast for me. But they sounded like men."

McNally made notes. "What time was this?"

"About fifteen, twenty minutes before you arrived."

McNally glanced at her watch and wrote down the time. "Do you know how they got in?"

"I think they broke in through the kitchen door. Back here." She led the way through the narrow path in the living room and into the kitchen. She pointed at the hole in the kitchen-door window and the glass on the floor.

McNally made notes. "Okay." She searched the area. "Have you had any issues like this before?" She turned and headed back to the living room.

"No." For a brief moment, her mind turned to her brother Cash. *Did he have something to do with this? Or one of his cohorts?* Surely not.

McNally searched the room again, distaste creeping onto her face. She spoke with hesitation. "Do...you know if...they took anything?"

Henny flushed. She *didn't* know. How could she? Her gaze trailed around the room and for the first time, briefly, she saw her space through the eyes of a stranger. "Uh, I, uh…" Her voice shook with emotion. The emotion of embarrassment choking out the fear and anger from the intrusion. "I don't know." She crossed her arms over her middle. "I'm sorry. I guess this was a waste of your time."

When the officer left, Henny pulled out a piece of cardboard and duct tape. She patched the hole in the kitchen-door window and swept up the glass. As she swept, she pushed aside a box, swept, relocated a pile of books, swept, moved a plastic container, swept. With each item she shifted, Henny grew increasingly irritated with her inability to move freely. She just wanted to sweep up the blasted glass! She opened the kitchen door and, muttering to herself, began tossing boxes, bags, and books onto the screened porch.

"What are you doing?" Walter asked, appearing to sit in the wicker chair stationed in the corner of the porch. "Are you okay?"

"I'm fine," Henny snipped. "I'm getting this stuff out of my way so I can clean up the broken glass."

"Broken glass?"

"Yes." She planted her hand on her hip. "Someone broke in. Where were you?"

"Broke in? Who? When?"

"Tonight. Not even an hour ago."

"I guarantee it has something to do with Cash."

"I don't want to hear it right now." She threw a box into the corner.

"Are you throwing this stuff away?"

"No. I don't know. Maybe." The image of Prettie's bright and spacious living room invaded her mind. "I don't know what I'm doing right now. I just want some space."

She left Walter on the porch and slammed the kitchen door, her throat growing tight, on the verge of tears. Would she ever be happy, truly happy, again? Would this gaping hole right in her center ever be full again? She hoped Cash came home soon so she could question him about the break-in.

Henny swept the glass into the dust pan. The shards caught the light and glinted like sequins. She loved sparkly things. Henny dumped the glass into a shopping bag and tied the handles together. She held the bag over the garbage can, tension wrenching her shoulders. She lifted her arms and placed the bag on top of the refrigerator.

13

As soon as Henny woke up the next morning, she was banging on Cash's bedroom door. "Get up! I want to talk to you!"

Walter appeared behind her. "Are you kicking him to the curb?"

"Not now, Walter," she hissed.

A few minutes later, Cash jerked open the door, bleary-eyed, hair sticking up as he tied his robe. "What do you want?"

"Someone broke into my house last night. Do you know anything about it?"

"Why would I break into the house? I have a key." He leaned against the doorjamb.

"I didn't say *you* did it, ya fool. I'm wondering if it's one of your idiot friends." She made air quotes around the word "friends."

He squinted at her. "What? Why would they?"

"That's what I want to know."

"Henny, I don't know what you're talking about. I don't know who would've broken in here or why."

"Did you tell anybody I have money or anything? Which I don't. But did you mouth off and lead someone to believe it'd be a good idea to break in and steal stuff?"

He sighed. "I don't know. I don't think so."

"Fat lot of help you are." She turned and sidestepped down the hall, muttering to herself. "I wish you'd hurry up and get out of my house. I've had nothing but problems ever since you moved in."

"Is that it?" Walter said.

"Well, what else do you expect me to do? He said he's getting out as soon as he finds a place to live and a job."

"He's a squatter!" Walter shouted, glowing brightly.

Cash was following her. "Who are you talking to?"

Henny froze and stared at him like a deer in headlights. "I-uh-I'm talking to you."

He narrowed his eyes in disbelief. "Nah. I don't think you were. It seemed like you were talking to someone else. Do you have the dementia or something?"

"No, I don't have no dadburned dementia. What I have is a big pain in the butt!"

Cash looked at her, puzzled, and stepped into the bathroom for his shower.

Henny made cinnamon rolls and coffee and camped in her recliner to watch the morning news. The anchor, a handsome middle-aged man neatly dressed in a suit, announced, "Thirty-eight year old Jacob Arnold and forty-two year old Gibson Pinnette were arrested early this morning in a real-estate fraud scheme."

As the anchor spoke, images of Jake Arnold and another man, both in handcuffs being led from their homes, flashed across the screen. Henny lowered her cinnamon roll and sat up to gape at the television. "Oh, my stars," she whispered. "I can't believe it."

The anchor continued, "Pinnette, a home inspector, falsified home inspections, causing homebuyers to buy damaged homes unawares. His co-conspirator, Arnold, then gave him a share of his commission. The two men will face charges of fraud, wire fraud, and conspiracy, among other charges. Both men are being held on ten thousand dollars bail."

Well, nothing was said about murder, however. Surely if the police thought Jake Arnold was implicated in Leyla's murder, that would be announced too.

A knock sounded at the front door, causing her to jump. A front-door knock meant either an acquaintance who hadn't yet made it into friend status, or a stranger.

"Hold on a minute," Henny shouted. She struggled to lock the footstool into place as Cash rushed past her to answer the door, smelling fresh with cologne.

She finally got on her feet and jammed them into the bunny slippers as a blast of cold November air swept into the room when Cash opened the door. Sheriff Basham in his puffy uniform coat and a lean dark-haired woman entered the room. Henny ran her eyes over the stranger-woman who, a full foot shorter than Basham, wore a rumpled navy suit and was holding a padfolio against her chest. Her dark hair was pulled into a tight ponytail, and at least three sleepless nights weighed down her eyes. She was clearly some sort of official.

Basham took off his sunglasses and tucked them in the neck of his shirt. "Good morning, Mrs. Wiley. I'm sorry if I woke you."

Henny said, "I'm so glad you're here. I just saw on the news where Jake Arnold was arrested for fraud. Did you find any connection to Leyla Hager's murder too? I mean, I heard Jake and Leyla had been fighting. Maybe he killed her."

Amusement lit his hard eyes. "As you well know, Mrs. Wiley, I'm not able to discuss the details of his case or our investigation with you. But I assure you we are looking carefully at all evidence and suspects in Mrs. Hager's case."

"Can you at least tell me if you're actually making any head-way? Or if anyone is standing out as the possible killer? I mean, I'm concerned about a killer running the streets of this town. It's scary."

"Of course, I do understand your concern, ma'am. We are making progress in the investigation; there are a couple of people we are especially interested in. I really can't tell you more."

Well, that was no help. Henny crossed her arms.

Basham continued. "However, we are here for different rea-sons today." He motioned to the woman beside him. "I'd like you to meet Mrs. Juanita Lopez from Adult Services. We're here on a welfare check."

It was like a punch in the face. Henny staggered back a cou-ple of steps and put her hand on a stack of boxes to steady herself.

Mrs. Lopez took in the room from corner to corner, ceiling to floor, her face straining against her true feelings. Henny knew all too well a face struggling to hide disgust and pity. Ire and a deep, painful shame like shards of glass flew up in Henny's chest and crept up her throat, into her face, and made the roots of her hair burn. She *hated* anyone outside the family being inside her home, seeing her most intimate secret, her soul laid bare.

Henny glowered at Cash. She slapped his arm. "What is wrong with you? Why'd you let them in? Being a jailbird, you'd think you'd know something about the Fourth Amendment," she muttered, adding, "Addle-brained jackrabbit."

"Mrs. Wiley, we are only here to help you," she said in a softly accented voice, offering her a business card.

Henny stared at the card, refusing to accept it. Instead, she ran her fingers to settle her bed-hair. "I don't recall asking for help."

"I'll just place it here." Lopez placed the card on top of the recliner. "We've received reports about the..." Lopez paused, clearly selecting her word choice. "...condition of your home."

Henny glared at her, her face swollen and hot from her blood pressure building. She could feel her heartbeat in her cheeks. "Reports from who?"

"We like to keep that confidential because it's irrelevant to the primary issue, which is—"

"Irrelevant!" Henny shouted. "It's not irrelevant to me. You're telling me I have an enemy out in the world putting a target on my back, and I'm not allowed to know who's trying to take me down? I have a right to know—" She fixed her attention on Basham. "You! You did this to me!"

Basham held up his hand, humor shining in his eyes. "Mrs. Wiley. I think you're overreacting a little. No one is out to get you. This is all for your safety. Besides, I was not the only one to report."

"I'm not overreacting! This is *my* house in these United States, and I'm allowed to live however I want. And just because some nosey Rosie can't mind their business... Wait..." Henny paused and stared at Basham and Lopez as the realization dawned on her. She stuck out her chin and crossed her arms over her chest. "Gloria Hatfield." She nodded. "Gloria Stinking Hatfield reported me, didn't she?"

Mrs. Lopez pinched her lips into a patient smile. "We can't reveal any information about who reported you. But we would like to offer to help you clean up and improve your situation. While it's true that you can live mostly however you want in the US, there are limitations when it threatens your health and safety or the health and safety of others."

Chomping down on her anger, Henny cut her eyes at her brother Cash, who gaped between Henny and the visitors. "You know, Henny, she's not exactly wrong. I mean..." He motioned around the room. "It's kind of a mess in here."

She scowled at him, then turned back to the visitors. "Get. Out," Henny snarled, snatching the business card Lopez had offered and ripping it to shreds as she chanted, "Getoutgetoutgetout. I don't need you. I don't want you here."

"Mrs. Wiley," Basham interrupted her exorcism.

Henny stared at him, balling the shredded business card in her fist.

"We've been called here for a welfare check, and we can't leave until we have a plan to ensure your safety."

Lopez said, "Unfortunately, judging by the current condition of your home, you are in grave danger should an emergency occur."

The sticky sweetness of Lopez's demeanor made Henny want to launch herself on this woman and claw her face. "I'm not a child or an idiot," Henny said. "Stop talking to me in that kindergarten teacher voice before I—" Henny stopped herself before she said *before I slap it right out of your mouth.* She was speaking to a government official and wasn't in the mood to be arrested. The room was growing hotter and the walls were closing in. She struggled to breathe, and her eyes stung, pushing back on the tears threatening to spill. Her skin prickled. Is this what possession felt like?

Basham stepped up to shield Lopez. "Ma'am, I'd hate for this friendly visit to get ugly. But that's up to you."

Lopez put her hand on his arm and stepped from behind him. "It's okay, Sheriff. I've seen this before. Mrs. Wiley is feeling a little threatened and defensive right now. With good reason.

It's difficult to process this situation." Lopez turned back to Henny and said in a less-sweet tone, "You must get this cleaned up, because, when we pulled up, I noticed it's beginning to spread into the yard. You are creating a hazard not only for yourself, but for your neighbors, and we can't allow that."

"Get out," Henny said, looking at the crooked ears on her bunny slippers.

"I'll give you some time to calm down. I'll be in touch next week to start the cleanup process. I think it would be best for you if we can get it done before winter sets in and all the critters start looking for places to hide. Also, you might incur heavy fines if—"

Henny spoke louder. "Get. Out."

Lopez said, "Mrs. Wiley—"

Henny shouted, "Get! Out! Get out of my house!" She pointed at Basham. "Both of you. You have no right being here any longer. Leave!" She threw the shredded business card at Lopez. It hit her in the chest and fluttered to the floor in pieces.

Basham lowered his head. "Very well." He motioned toward the front door. "Ma'am, it's time to go." Mrs. Lopez started to speak, and he cut her off. "Nope. Time to go." He opened the front door. "C'mon, now. We've fulfilled our purpose here." He guided her out the door and paused on the threshold. "Mr. Cooper, while I'm here, are you busy today?"

Cash's brows shot up. "I planned on looking for a job today."

Basham nodded. "Before you do that, I need you to stop by the station. I have more questions regarding the murder of Leyla Hager."

Cash looked at Henny as if to say *I told you so.*

"I didn't do anything. I don't know what happened after she dropped me off."

"I understand. I just have a few more questions. It'll go smoother for all of us if you cooperate so things don't get ugly."

"We can do it now."

Basham pushed his bottom lip upward. "Mm. I think it'd be best to do it at the station."

Concern marked Cash's face. He glanced at Henny. Henny looked down at her bunny slippers. He said, "All right. I'll be out there directly."

Basham stepped through the door, saying to Lopez, "Let's go. We don't want to overstay our welcome."

"Too late!" Henny slammed the door on them and locked it. Tears slipped down her cheeks. She sniffled and wiped her eyes. Anger pulsed through her body. "Lord, help me," she whispered.

Cash said, "Henny..."

"Don't talk to me right now." She swiped her arm through the air. "I can't even look at you." She picked her way through the living room. She started down the hallway. "Don't ever let those people inside this house again. Not ever." She stopped and turned. "But then I expect I won't need to worry much about it, because you ain't going to be around here much longer."

"Henny—"

She lifted her hand to stop him. "You'd better get dressed and get to work finding a home and a job. You don't have time to spare."

He tipped his head, puzzled.

"You have one week to get out of my house."

She turned to continue down the hall to her collection room. Cash called after her, but she ignored him. She pulled some clothes out of the collection room. She touched the red glittery shoe on the top of the pile on the bed, which usually made her feel better. But, this time, it didn't. She carried herself to the bathroom, pushed some perfume and cosmetics bottles and jars aside to clear a spot to lay her clothes. She dragged herself into a hot shower, the faces of Lopez and Basham haunting her. How dare they come into her home, call it a mess—a *hazard*!—and then tell her she must clean it up or "incur heavy fines." Henny scrubbed her skin pink with the loofah and rose-scented suds, grumbling to herself about the annoying visit.

Once out of the shower, she fixed her hair and makeup, put on her cozy gray fleece shirt and blue jeans, but still didn't feel any better. In fact, she couldn't stop thinking about the interaction and only felt worse: more hurt, more angry, more...betrayed.

She marched into the kitchen where Cash sat, dressed in his all-black garb, pecking around on his laptop. She reached for a mug and the coffee pot. No coffee. Of course. She growled, slammed the carafe into its home. She shoved her feet into her shoes, grabbed her jacket and keys.

"When will you be back?" Cash asked.

She slammed the door and stormed across the yard to her truck. The wind shook the trees, brightly colored leaves swirling to the ground, and heavy gray clouds pressed down on the horizon. It was probably going to rain today. She started up the truck. Walter appeared in the seat beside her. "What's up, hon? Why're you sad?"

"I don't want to talk about it." Honestly, she *did* want to talk about it. But she knew she'd burst into tears the moment she began to speak. She was fragile, barely holding herself together.

"Where're you going?"

She put the truck into gear and began to back out. "To the only place that will make me feel better."

"Aw, you aren't going diving again, are you?"

His remark was a knife in the gut, twisting the threads of her misery into a hard, sticky knot, like a wad of taffy.

"What's it matter to you?"

"Don't you have enough stuff?"

She didn't want to hear this from him too—even if it was true. She whipped the truck into the street and pressed the gas pedal. Walter, not able to leave the property for some ghost reason she didn't understand, disappeared. She aimed her truck toward the Hobby Hut. She didn't care that it was first thing in the morning. They wouldn't be open for another hour anyway. Just the act of digging for treasure would unwind her swirling thoughts and bring down her blood pressure. When she dug for treasures, it was like floating on water on a sunny day, warm and cozy, her mind settling into a contented buzz.

Henny whipped into the empty parking lot of the Plumridge Plaza and pulled up behind the Hobby Hut, where one of her favorite dumpsters sat. Maybe there would be some Halloween decorations she could use next year or something broken for Thanksgiving or Christmas that could be easily fixed. The thought of such delights began to lift her mood like wind billowing sheets on a clothing line. She slipped from her truck, grabbed her glittery bag out of the back, and marched to the dumpster. She grasped the handle and stopped. The voices of Walter, Ida Mae, Cash, Mrs. Lopez, and Basham all rushed toward her, pounding against her mind and her heart. If all those people were saying she was too messy, had too many things, maybe they were right?

Tears stung her eyes. She did have a lot of things, if she was being honest with herself. But she needed those things. Her collections, some of them, had been gathered over a lifetime. Though, granted, most of them came after her daughter, Lydia, sweet, precious Lydia, her baby girl, had died so many years ago and left a hole inside her that never really filled up. And then Walter had died about five years ago, making the hole deeper and wider. Henny dropped her hand. Is that what all this treasure hunting was about? Trying to fill up that hole? She turned her back to the dumpster and slid down to sit on a crate. Would that hole ever be filled? She dropped her face into her hands and cried.

14

enny no longer had the heart for diving today. She gathered up her diving kit and dropped it in the back of her truck. Her head ached from the heavy emotions and lack of caffeine. She left the plaza and went home for a big cup of coffee to knock the chill off her bones.

Her cell phone rang. Keeping her eyes on the road, she dug in her purse to retrieve it. When she answered, Sheriff Basham said, "Mrs. Wiley, I have a few more questions for you. I was wondering if you could come to the station at your earliest convenience."

"Is this about my brother?"

He didn't answer her question, but asked his own. "Are you available this afternoon?"

"I'll be there in about ten minutes." At the next stop light, she made a U-turn and headed toward the sheriff's department.

She stepped into the station, blinking against the fluorescent lights. Sheriff Basham held the door open for her and escorted her to an interview room. "I won't keep you long. I just had a few questions about the purse you found and turned in to my deputy."

"Okay."

He opened the door and showed her inside, saying, "Would you like a cup of coffee?"

"Yes, please." She settled at a table, clutching her purse in her lap as she looked around the room.

A few moments later, he came back with two Styrofoam cups of coffee and joined her at the table. He pulled out a pad of paper and a pen. "So, let's review. You found the dead body and then later happened to also find the deceased's purse."

Henny couldn't ignore the edge of accusation in his voice. "Yes."

"And where did you find the purse?"

"In a dumpster behind Luxe Locks Salon."

He studied her. "What made you think to look there for the purse?"

"I wasn't looking for the purse. It was an accident."

He nodded, stabbing his paper with the tip of his pen. "I think you can see my issue. *You* find the body. *You* happen to also find the purse. Your brother is one of the last people to see her alive..." His voice trailed off.

Henny grew rigid and stared at him as the wheels in her mind processed his insinuation. "Wait a hot minute. Are you *accusing* me of something? Because if you are, you really need to come on out and say it."

"It seems fishy to me. Maybe you're helping your brother cover up his crime."

Henny launched from her seat. "What? Are you out of your pointy-headed mind? I would never—" Her mind wheeled. "I cannot believe you—" She couldn't even form or express a complete, coherent thought.

"Please, have a seat. We're just talking. That's all."

Henny eased into her seat. "Look, sometimes, when I get anxious..." Shame burned in her face and spread into her chest. She didn't like talking about her pastime with people. "I like to rummage through dumpsters around town. It's where I find a lot of my treasures."

"You really shouldn't be doing that."

She didn't need any of his judgments. "It doesn't hurt anyone and it makes me happy. Anyway, I was treasure-hunting and I happened upon the purse. It was purely accidental."

He nodded again and stopped pecking the paper with his pen. He stared at her. "Yet, when you found the body, you never mentioned a thing about your brother, Cash, being on a date with her that night. You must've known about it."

Oh, no. Panic fluttered through Henny like pheasants flushing from a bush. "It's not what you think."

He leaned forward, crowding her. "I hope not. Because what I'm thinking is your brother killed Leyla Hager and you helped him cover it up. Is that what happened?"

"No! Nonononono! I didn't tell you anything about their date because of his past. He's trying to get his life back on track. So, I wanted to see what I could find out because Cash is *not* a killer. He's a thief and a conman and a complete weasel, but he is not a murderer. I was afraid y'all wouldn't be able to look at him objectively and fairly."

"I'm sorry you feel that way. I've worked hard to protect this community and put people like your brother behind bars when they commit crimes."

"I understand that, and I appreciate the work you and your deputies do. But my brother didn't kill Leyla Hager. I mean, didn't y'all find some fingerprints or DNA or something on her purse?"

"We have to wait awhile to get any DNA hits, but we did find prints. We found Leyla's, of course. And we found another set of prints. We're waiting to see if they match Cash's. You'd better hope they don't. Because if his fingerprints are on the purse, then we have cause to suspect you as an accessory to his crime and maybe even obstruction. That you were trying to put us off Cash and redirect our attention elsewhere."

Henny's mind buzzed. Thinking straight was impossible now. "That's not what happened. And what about Susan Elsher? She attacked Leyla. I saw it. She yelled at her, shoved her, and threatened her. Or-or-or what about Jake Arnold? The receptionist at the real estate firm said he and Leyla had argued over some sort of shady dealings he was involved in and was just arrested for."

His eyes flashed. "Are you certain?"

"About eighty percent sure."

"Hm. Well..." He tapped his paper with his pen. "At any rate, we're going to talk to Mrs. Elsher again..." He wrote down the name Jake Arnold on his paper. "And I'll have another chat with Mr. Arnold."

Henny didn't want to be here anymore. The walls of the room seemed to be closing in. "Am I under arrest?"

"No."

She jumped up. "Then you can't keep me. I'm leaving." She headed for the door. "I don't know who killed Leyla, but it wasn't my brother; and, I promise you, if he *did* do something so evil, I'd turn him in myself."

Henny rushed to her truck, her hands shaking as she opened the door and started the engine. She blew out a breath and, clutching the steering wheel, dropped her head to rest on it, trying to steady her nerves. When she'd regained a semblance of calm, she fled from the sheriff's department. She still wasn't clear about who might've had a hand in Leyla's murder. The names kept mounting, but none of them stood out as the prime suspect. She hoped the killer would be discovered soon. Her nerves couldn't take much more of this.

15

The phone was ringing as Henny stepped into the house. The house was otherwise quiet and dark, indicating that Cash was gone. She grabbed the phone. It was Ida Mae.

Forgoing typical telephone etiquette, Ida Mae just started talking in the way the sisters had grown accustomed to. "I found out the details for Leyla's funeral."

"Oh, good. I was going to call Prettie this afternoon." She set her stuff down and moved toward the coffee pot, pulling out the canister, filters, and a mug.

"Visitation at the Curtis Funeral Home is tomorrow. Then Prettie is having a wake over at the house with closest family and friends. She wants us to come, if we can. I told her we'd bring food. I'm bringing fried corn and honey-baked ham if you want to bring your pumpkin pecan cake. The one with the maple frosting."

"Oh, yeah. Okay. I can do that." She placed a filter in the coffee pot and scooped in coffee. "What time is the visitation?"

"Around noon until three or so. Then we'll all go over to Prettie's for the wake. The funeral will be the following morning, out at the Memorial Gardens Cemetery."

"Oh, that's a pretty place. I'll need to set an appointment to get my hair done." She pulled the tin foil off the chocolate cherry cola cake with buttercream frosting and maraschino cherries and removed a saucer from the cabinet.

"Shoot! Me too. Hope we can get in first thing."

"Let me go now so I'll call out there to see if she can squeeze us in."

Henny paused her snack preparations to call the Sassy Styles Salon. Fortunately, she was able to secure a trim and style for her and Ida Mae for eight in the morning. She wrote it on the calendar beside the fridge and called Ida Mae back to tell her. She cut off a big chunk of cake while the phone rang. The scent of coffee filled the air.

When Ida Mae answered, Henny said, "I have us scheduled for eight in the morning, so be dressed and ready to go."

"All right."

"It's been a heckuva morning, let me tell you." Henny sat at the table with her cake and coffee and spilled all the tea about the events of the morning.

"I cannot believe the sheriff and that woman ambushed you like that. Why did Cash let them in the house?"

"Because he's a moron." She took a big bite of cake and spoke as she chewed. "I don't think I need to clean up, but if I did, I wouldn't even know where to begin."

"You want my help?"

"I don't know." Henny looked around the room at the boxes, bags, books, newspapers, and magazines and such stacked everywhere. She shoved another piece of cake in her mouth: maybe that would clear up the pile of gravel that seemed to be clogging her esophagus. "I don't like the idea of some outsider coming into my home, telling me how to live."

"It's for your own good and well-being in the end, though."

Henny grunted. "I happen to think that me being left alone is for my good and well-being."

Ida Mae laughed. "Well, if you want any help, you just let me know."

"I wouldn't even know where to begin."

"Like eating an elephant, Sis. One room at a time, one piece at a time. Though, if I was you, I'd start outside since your neighbor Gloria has already reported you." A bit of silence passed between them as Henny sipped her coffee and rolled around the idea of cleaning up her house. "You think Susan had anything to do with Leyla's death?"

"I don't know. She's meaner than a rattlesnake, I'll tell you that. And a drinker."

"You mean a drunk?"

"Oh yeah. Which is probably what makes her so blasted mean." Henny chewed a chunk of chocolatey cherry cake. "I don't think I've ever wanted to slap a woman so bad in my life."

Ida Mae paused. "Maybe she had too much to drink, got into it with Leyla, and killed her by accident."

"Maybe. And then drove her car out to that old gas station and set it on fire to hide the evidence."

"Crazier things have happened for less."

"True words there."

"What about Cash? What did he say when you told him to get out?"

"He didn't say anything. But he's not here right now. And I mean it, Ida Mae. I'll put his stuff in the yard and set it on fire if he ain't out of here in one week."

Ida Mae laughed. "Oh, Henny. You don't mean that."

Henny puffed up. Maybe she did, maybe she didn't. "We'll find out in a week, won't we?"

The sisters said their goodbyes, and Henny sat at the table, fin-ishing her cake and coffee, taking in the scene around her. Maybe she didn't need to get rid of anything. Maybe if she just...organized her stuff, it would be enough to get the sheriff and Mrs. Lopez off her back. The best of both worlds, right? She keeps her stuff. She makes the officials happy. And everyone gets off her back about the mess. Maybe she could even have visitors inside. Her shoul-ders rose up to her ears as though a wrench had torqued them into place. Maybe not visitors *inside*. That was awfully *intimate*, having people inside the home. A wave of heat rippled through her, and a thin film of sweat broke out on her palms and between her breasts. She fanned herself with a nearby paper plate. It was too much to even think about. She blew out a breath. *One thing at a time, Henny. One thing at a time.* Her coffee and cake finished, she put her dishes in the sink and turned to search the room.

"What could I move? And where could I put it?" She could move a couple of those boxes along the wall, but she needed to go through them first. That was too much right now. She could go through the shopping bags next to the boxes. It should be easier since the bags weren't as big and didn't contain as much stuff. Regardless, she still needed to go through everything and find a place for all the items. The thought of doing that weighed like an anchor against her. It was too much to think about and carry out. There. A rusty *Wizard of Oz* lunchbox she'd purchased from an estate sale a few months ago. She could store it in her collec-tion room with her other *Wizard of Oz* items.

Feeling good about her decision, she carried the box to the collection room. She picked her way through the boxes, bags, and kickbacks on the floor, making her way to the bookshelf in the corner loaded with a variety of books, *Wizard of Oz* dolls, figurines, and other ornaments. She moved a couple of items around, scraping them through the dust on the wood. "Whew! I need to dust in here." She placed the lunchbox front and center over the non-dusty spots she'd just cleared.

She paused and looked down. On the bottom shelf was a clear space of wood in the shape of a rectangle of about six inches by four inches, with some dust around the clearing. She frowned. Something was missing. Looking around, Henny didn't see anything nearby that might've been knocked off the shelf. Then again, it was kind of difficult to tell with so many things lying around. But there wasn't anything nearby that fit the shape of the spot left in the dust on the shelf.

This was confusing. What had been there? She had so much stuff... She slammed the door on that thought. It sounded too much like all the accusations leveled at her over the years from Walter and Ida Mae—an irritating refrain that never seemed to end: *Too much stuff. Too much stuff.* But what was missing and where did it go? Maybe she did have too much stuff if she couldn't remember what she had. Maybe she'd moved something around... *No.* She didn't move things. Cash. This had to somehow come back on him. She frowned.

Maybe he'd been nosing around in here and had moved it. Or maybe he'd stolen it. But why? She didn't have anything worth stealing. She looked around the room. This stuff was really only valuable to herself.

Walter popped into the room, humming "Hunk of Burning Love." In his best Elvis impersonation, which really wasn't good, he said, "Hey there, darling. What's shakin'?"

"What are you doing here? I thought you were boycotting the house until Cash moved out."

"He's not here right now. Good enough. I've been coming in and out whenever he leaves. I don't like being run out of my own house. Besides, it's boring in the tree." He lit up his pipe. The cherry vanilla scent soothed Henny. "Whatcha doing?" he asked.

"I'm wondering what was there." She pointed to the bottom shelf.

He scratched the back of his head, adjusted his John Deere cap, and tucked his thumbs in the sides of his bib overalls. "Lord. Could've been anything."

She rolled her eyes. "I know that. Do you remember what it was?"

"How the heck should I know? I never came in this room when I was alive, and once I was dead I didn't get more interested in it. Too crowded."

She crossed her arms. "Did you happen to see Cash nosing around in here or taking anything out of here?"

He thought. "Seems I did see him taking a box out a couple of days ago."

Henny gaped at him. "Did you see what was in the box?"

"Nah. I didn't pay any attention to what it was. I thought that he might be finally moving out. Why?"

"I can't prove it yet, but I think he's the one who took whatever was in that spot."

"I don't know why you care. Most of this stuff ain't even worth burning."

She frowned. "*You* might not think this stuff is worth anything, but *I* do."

"I know. It's your treasure." He sighed and put his arm around her. Obviously, she couldn't feel his touch, only a cold tingling where his arm would be if he were alive. She wished there was some comfort in it, but there wasn't. In fact, it only made her miss him more.

"So, I popped in to tell you that I saw that woman you asked me about. I tried to talk to her, but she couldn't speak. She kept grabbing her throat and moving her lips. If I had to guess, I'd say she'd been strangled."

"My goodness! Is she always going to be like that?"

"Nah. We eventually get restored to our perfect form, even better than we were before."

"Eventually?"

"I guess perfection takes time."

"How long does it take?"

"I have no idea. Could take hundreds of years, for all I know. It doesn't matter how long it takes, I guess. I mean, what else am I doing?"

She looked at him and smiled. "I hope you're not in your perfect form yet. I remember when you were buffer and had more hair."

They laughed. "Me, too," he said. "Surely, I have more progress to make. Maybe I'm still"—he made air quotes with his fingers—"baking."

They laughed again. "I wish I understood how things work on your side."

"Me too!" He chuckled.

Henny sighed. "I miss ya, you old coot."

"I miss you, too, you old hen."

They shared another laugh. Henny smiled at him, wishing she could rest her head on his shoulder. She hadn't shared a laugh with him in a long time.

Henny said, "Well, I don't have time to mess with whatever

this missing thing is right now. I have a cake to bake and have to run out to get some supplies. I'll deal with this later. If Leyla ever speaks, let me know. Especially if she tells you anything about her death."

"I sure will."

Henny left the room filled with an aching loneliness and a sense of hope. Even though Walter had left her alone in this life, there was hope for their reunion one day.

16

enny jumped in the truck, shaking off the chill and the rain, and headed out to grab a few items to make the pumpkin cake for the wake tomorrow. On her way to the grocery store, she noticed a little boutique, To the Nines, nestled across the street in a white brick building with a pink-and-white striped awning. Pretty dresses on dressmaker mannequins lined the windows like confections. Even though she probably had a dress at home, it might be nice to have a new one for the funeral or wake. Plus, she'd never been in that boutique before. She'd heard good things about it from the women at church, though.

A bell chimed as Henny entered the boutique. The scent of verbena and lime met her and pulled her deeper inside the building outfitted in a blend of modern and Victorian decor. A few women and girls circled the racks. The clerk, a young girl with sleek dark hair, assisted a customer. That was Jill, Susan's daughter. What a small world! Jill didn't seem to notice Henny, but that was okay. She didn't really need any help. She made her way to a rack of dresses better suited to her age and picked through them. She found a simple dark navy dress with a boat neck, three-quarter sleeves, and slight A-line skirt.

"Isn't that cute?" Henny muttered, holding up the dress to examine it and to hold it over her chest to gauge the length.

"Hi, can I help you?" Jill asked.

"Oh, no. I'm okay. Thanks, hon."

The girl squinted and pointed at Henny. "Aren't you the lady who was at my house earlier?"

"Yup." She held up her hands. "But I'm not following you. I promise. It's pure coincidence. I just wanted to come in and see what y'all had. I've never been here. It's super cute. I was hoping to find a dress for a funeral."

"I'm sorry to hear that. Would it happen to be Luke's mom?" She slouched, picking at her nails. "She's the only person I've heard of dying recently. But I guess that's a stupid question. I mean, like, people die every day, right?"

"You're right. People do die every day. But you're also right about it being Luke's mom."

She flashed soft brown eyes at her. "I really liked her."

Part of Henny was just making conversation with a girl who seemed lonely and seemed to desperately need a kind word. But, admittedly, the other part was digging for information. Two birds, one stone. "Did you know her well?"

"Not super-close, Luke and I hung out over at his dad's house when Ruskin had Luke for his weekends. Leyla seemed really nice, but she and Ruskin fought a lot. Luke was pretty embarrassed by it."

"It's hard when parents don't get along."

"I know all about that." She rolled her eyes.

"I heard your mom say Leyla gave you advice?"

"Yeah. Not a lot, though. I only saw her for a few minutes when she came to pick up Luke. But she's the one who persuaded me to join the cheer squad."

"Really?"

Her face lit up. "Oh, yeah. I was really nervous about it and wasn't sure I could do it, but she said being a cheerleader was the best time of her life when she was younger. She said that even though it was hard, it could change my life in wonderful ways."

"Why didn't your mom want you to be a cheerleader?"

She shrugged a shoulder. "I don't know. Lots of reasons. Money. It can be pretty expensive with camps and traveling and stuff. My grades. And I think she had some bad experiences with some cheerleaders when she was in school, so she thinks they're all horrible people forever, I guess." She scoffed. "I don't know. I'm just, like, whatever, Mom."

"I'm sure her heart is in the right place." Though, to be honest, Henny wasn't sure the woman had a heart. There was probably a box of wine in its place.

"I guess." Jill made a face as though she didn't quite believe it. "I feel so sorry for Luke, though, you know? His dad is, like, a major jerk and then his mom dies? And not just dies, but is *murdered*. That's, like, the worst luck ever, right?"

"Sounds like you know him pretty well."

She flushed a sheepish grin meant only for girls crushing hard on a boy. "Yeah, for sure." She tucked her hair behind her ears. "He goes to my school. We're in algebra together. He's really smart. Which you wouldn't think he would be because he's also super popular and plays lots of sports. Everyone likes him. He's nice to everyone."

"I don't know him too well, but I'm pretty good friends with his Aunt Prettie. He sounds like a special guy." Henny hoped for this girl's sake that Susan and Rusk didn't get married. It would be weird for her to crush on her new stepbrother.

"He is." The dopey grin crossed her face again and she picked at her nails.

Henny glanced at her nails. Glittery purple with a silver star. Henny blinked. She'd seen that exact design before. At the abandoned gas station where she'd found Leyla's body. "I, uh, like your nails. Really pretty." She and Amber both had the same style. She studied Jill. There was no way she was involved. She was far too sweet. But, come to think of it, Amber was sweet too. Or so Henny had thought. That is, until she saw Amber at the sheriff's department. So maybe Jill wasn't as gentle as she thought. Or, worse, maybe they were *both* involved somehow.

"Thanks." She held them out to admire them. "Just got them done. All of us have them to go with our uniforms."

"All of you, who?"

"The cheerleaders at Plumridge High."

"That's cool." Henny wanted desperately to ask her about the nail she found at the murder scene, but she didn't know how to approach it without the conversation getting really weird, really fast.

Jill looked at Henny's dress. "You know what would be super-cute with that dress?" She walked across the floor to the accessories section and picked up a square of cloth. She unfolded a paisley pashmina shawl with navy, purple, and fuchsia and carried it back to Henny. "Put this around your shoulders. Pin it with a pearl brooch. Super cute."

She was right. Henny touched the soft shawl. "And it would be warm if the church is cool and walking around outside at the gravesite."

"Totally." Jill wrapped the shawl around the dress. "See?"

"I love it."

"I can ring you up unless you need anything else?"

Henny's hand itched as she searched the space for something else she couldn't live without. But Mrs. Lopez's face flashed in her mind. The room grew warmer, the lights brighter, and the music louder. The sure signs of sensory overload. She needed some fresh air. "No. That's okay. I think I'm set."

Henny and Jill sidled up to the counter, and Jill began ringing up the sale. The bell at the door chimed. Jill looked up, and the smile faded from her face. A look of panic and distrust filled her eyes, and her body tensed as though she was preparing to fight or run.

Henny followed the direction of her gaze to see Amber and another girl enter the store. They stared at Jill with an air of menace. It was like one of those old westerns where the gunslingers took their stand, prepared to shoot their opponent. A snide smile crept over Amber's face. Then her eyes dropped to Henny and her face softened. Henny watched in amazement as the girl's face transformed in a flash.

Amber turned to her friend, said something, and they giggled. Then they moved over to a table of neatly folded shirts. They pulled up every one of them, pretending to look at them and dropped them in a wad on the table or the floor.

Henny turned to Jill. "Maybe you should call the police?"

Shaking, Jill zapped the price tags with the scan gun. "No, that's okay. It'll only make things worse. Your dress was on clearance, so the total is forty dollars and sixty cents."

Henny handed over her card, sneaking a glance at the girls pulling fashion jewelry off the pegs and dropping them on the ground or throwing them on a nearby table. Her blood began to heat up. She wasn't going to let this go without at least saying something. "Amber! That's your name, isn't it?"

Amber looked at her with cool defiance, but remained silent.

"That's right. I remember who you are. You're dating the nephew of one of my friends. And just you wait until I tell her how bratty you're acting. I can't believe she'd let her nephew continue dating someone like you."

Amber's eyes glittered with malice. "You don't know what you're talking about. Maybe you should ask Jill to tell you why I'm here. She knows."

Henny glanced at Jill. "Do you know what she's talking about?"

Jill flushed and shook her head. "She's delusional. But somehow it's my fault."

Amber laughed. "Oh, honey. I'm not the one who's delusional. More than one person has told me what you've been up to with Luke."

Uh-oh. Henny was deeper into a situation than she wanted to be. She did not want to be in between a couple of jealous girls fighting over a boy. But too late. She'd already opened her mouth. "Well, there's a way to handle it like mature people instead of rolling up in here and messing up the whole store like a couple of little fools. I bet your mommas would be ashamed they didn't raise you any better."

Amber lifted her chin in defiance, the hate intensifying in her eyes. Then she glared at Jill and pointed her finger. "I'll deal with you later." The girls turned around, and Amber swiped some clothes off a table onto the floor on their way out the door.

"What a couple of brats!" Henny seethed, marching over to help pick up the mess.

"You don't have to do that. I'll get it." Jill smiled weakly. "It's what I get paid for, anyway."

"Nonsense." The fall-colored corduroy pants looked like

fallen leaves. Henny picked up the pile from the floor and set about stacking them neatly.

"You're so sweet." Jill moved over to the T-shirt table to fold them.

"Are you going to be okay here by yourself? Do you think you'll be safe?"

"Yeah. They're just trying to intimidate me."

"I don't mean to pry, because I know it isn't any of my business, but why are they after you?"

"Amber doesn't like me and Luke hanging out, or talking, or...anything. She keeps a tight leash on him. Or tries to."

Henny was hoping the girl would say more, but she didn't, and Henny didn't know her well enough to pry any further. "Maybe you should call the police or something. They seemed pretty serious to me."

Jill rolled her eyes. "Nah. I've been putting up with this for months. Amber's just jealous. But she's all talk. Likes to look tough in front of her friends. She's a bully. Mom says if I ignore her, she'll go away."

Henny searched the girl's face. She seemed calm and assured. There was nothing else she could do about the situation. The girl wasn't related to her or even the daughter of a good friend. It was completely out of her hands now. And ultimately it was just schoolgirl stuff. The same kind of junk Henny and other kids had to put up with when she was in school. "Okay. Well, I feel bad about leaving you..."

"It's okay. Totally."

"Just keep an eye out for them in case they return. And maybe text your mom and friends a lot tonight, so they can keep track of you."

Jill smiled and chuckled. "I'll be okay."

A knot formed in her stomach. *I hope so.* "Okay, if you're sure..." Henny picked up her bags.

"I am." Jill nodded. "Thanks for stopping by. Have a good night."

Henny didn't feel good about leaving the girl, but she had no choice. She stepped outside, the wind and mist whipping through the air. She searched the parking lot and didn't see the girls. However, she didn't know what vehicle they might've driven, so they could be waiting in the parking lot, waiting for Henny to leave so they could catch Jill alone and pounce on her.

She put her bags behind the truck seat and climbed inside. There was one thing she could try to do to protect the girl. She pulled her phone out of her purse and dialed the sheriff's station.

When the receptionist answered, she said, "Hey there, this is Henny Wiley. I was just out at the little boutique To The Nines. And there's a young woman who works there; her name is Jill. She's there by herself. A couple of girls came in, bullied her, and made a real mess of the store. I chased them off, but I'm afraid they'll come back. Can y'all send someone out here to check on her this evening?"

The receptionist took the information. "We can't send anyone immediately, but we'll try to look into the situation this as soon as we can."

That wasn't the best answer Henny could've hoped for. She'd hoped they would respond with a little more urgency. "Sometime this evening? Don't you think y'all should be a little more... concerned?"

"Ma'am, we're doing the best we can. All my officers are out on calls right now. We will look in on her as soon as possible."

Henny sighed, biting back the growl trying to rise in her throat. She didn't have any recourse. "All right."

Unsettled, she drove to the grocery store. She didn't have any choice but to leave Jill alone to deal with her teenager issues.

Henny pulled into the grocery-store parking lot, the wind rocking her truck. The cold front was rolling in something fierce. She stepped against the wind, holding the hood of her jacket over her head, her purse tucked under her arm like a football.

She stepped under the portico to grab a cart from the cart bay and spotted Amber and Luke several feet away. Luke wore a green grocer's apron and a name tag. Amber seemed to be giving him what-for. Amber had him backed against the brick wall, as he looked down at his shoes, his hands in his pockets. Her face was pink, and her lips snipped off a string of inaudible words as she pointed at him. She was clearly irate.

"That little girl shore is busy today," Henny muttered to herself. She hated to see this boy put through the woodchipper of this girl's mouth. So she approached the couple.

As she stepped nearer, she heard Amber say, "You promised you would help and now you're trying to back out on it like some kind of *coward*? All you have to do is—" She stopped and turned to Henny. She put on a smile and said, "Hey, can I help you with something?"

Henny blinked at her, surprised. Well, this was an interesting switch. She wasn't this nice when she was with Jill. This girl's moods switched off and on faster than a lightning bug's butt.

Luke glanced at Henny. "Hey, Mrs. Wiley."

"Hey, Luke. I'm surprised to see you working today since your mom died."

He shrugged a shoulder. "It takes my mind off of things. And I need the money."

Amber smiled sweetly, rubbing his back. "It's worse to just sit at home and wallow in grief, don't you think? I'm sure Leyla would've wanted it this way."

Henny narrowed her eyes at her. *What a little minx.* That was the nicest word she could think about her at the moment. And this phony sweetness-and-light routine was getting old fast. Henny wasn't about to let this girl get away with manipulating Luke this way. "You're just hell on wheels, aren't you? Is there anyone you haven't told off or deceived today?"

Luke looked up at Henny and suppressed a smile as Amber stared daggers at her. "Amber's pretty feisty sometimes. Who've you been telling off today?"

"Jill Elsher."

"Why?" He frowned at Amber.

"Because she has been causing problems for me, Luke. You should hear the things she says to me at cheer practice." She put on a sad face.

Honestly, Henny didn't know for certain what was going on with the girls and she didn't know either of the girls or their families well enough to insert herself in the drama. She left high school drama back in high school. Thank goodness. But, she could at least plant enough doubt in Luke's mind about his vixen girlfriend. Henny scoffed and said to Luke, "I hope you aren't buying what she's selling. This one right here is a big ol' gumbo pot of trouble. I'll tell you that right now." As she turned back to grab a cart, she added, "Better watch your back with that one."

"And nosy old women need to mind their business," Amber shouted.

Henny ignored her and wheeled her rickety buggy into the store as a blast of hot air hit her in the face when the doors swiped open. She grabbed maple flavoring, pecans, butter, and several extra cans of pumpkin. She dropped some extra cream cheese in the buggy too. This close to Thanksgiving and Christmas meant a shortage of pumpkin and cream cheese. And there would be several pumpkin rolls to make for friends or sell at the church's Christmas Bazaar.

Luke breezed by on his way to the back of the store. He stopped by the swinging doors. "Hey, Mrs. Wiley. I want to apologize for Amber. She..."

"It's okay, sweetie. It's not your fault."

He shrugged, clearly struggling for the right words. "She's going through a lot at home right now. So, when she gets upset, she takes it out on people sometimes. It's not her fault."

"Sweetie, your momma just died. You're the one going through a lot."

He nodded, his gaze growing distant. "Yeah, but... You know what I mean."

Henny knew she should stay out of the middle of this teenage drama, but the words were already spilling out of her mouth. "Sweetie, I'm thinking Amber is deceiving you and taking advantage of your kindness."

Surprise marked his features.

She lifted her hands. "I'm not trying to interfere. Ultimately, you have to do what you think is right. But I used to be a high school girl once, and one thing is sure: mean girls today are the same as they were back in my day. That doesn't change. She has certainly showed me her true colors today. If I was your momma..." She stopped herself when his sad eyes met hers. "Well...I'm not. Of course. I'm sorry. Anyway, I'm going to keep shopping. I'll see you at the wake tomorrow."

He sniffed. "Funny, you sound like my mom."

"What do you mean?"

"My mom and Amber didn't like each other. They tried to get along, but my mom was always trying to break us up."

"Why?"

"Because I gave Amber a promise ring."

Henny's brows shot up. "Really! I can imagine your momma would be upset about that."

"Yeah. She lost it." Then he said in a mock mom voice, "You're too young to marry. You have too much going for you right now. You need to go to college. What about your scholarship?"

"She has a point."

"I guess. But she didn't know Amber like I do."

A regular Romeo and Juliet. Amazing how little teenagers had changed. Shakespeare wrote that play back in the late 1500s, and over four hundred years later a very similar story was playing out right here in little ol' Plumridge. Henny tried to control her face to keep from rolling her eyes. She didn't want to speak ill of Amber anymore because that was a surefire method to turn Luke toward Amber. By maintaining a neutral stance, he was more likely to come around to the truth himself. Eventually. Hopefully before that little man-eater-in-training destroyed him. "I'm sure your mom was worried. That's what moms do."

"Yeah. Well, I gotta clock in. See ya tomorrow." He disappeared through the swinging doors.

Henny shook her head and rolled her buggy to the front to check out her items. *Poor kid.* That little girl had him wrapped around her finger. Upon leaving the grocery, she noticed Amber leaning against a red Chevy pickup truck, jacked up on wheels with chrome exhaust stacks behind the truck cab. The guy inside wore a knit cap and gray thermal shirt. He had a dark, neatly trimmed beard and seemed to have a slight, strappy build.

Amber leaned on the truck with her elbows, her hands framing her forehead like she had a headache as she spoke to the guy.

Henny made her way to her truck and slowly put the bags inside as she watched the little scene unfold.

Amber stepped back as the guy opened the door. He slid from the truck, pulling up his saggy jeans. He lowered his truck gate, jumped up in the back, and pulled something toward the open tailgate. It seemed heavy, whatever it was. He jumped down and pulled a big black utility box out of the back.

Henny pushed her empty cart across the parking lot to the cart bay, keeping one eye on Amber and the stranger.

Amber pulled a set of keys out of her jacket pocket and walked toward another car in the parking lot. It was a light blue Toyota Corolla with a Plumridge High School sticker on the bumper. She opened the trunk, and the guy put the container inside. They stood talking for a moment as she shut the trunk. He returned to his truck, and she walked around to the driver's side of the Corolla.

Henny stood at her truck, her hand on the door, watching them. Amber stopped, turned, and looked right at Henny.

For a moment, Henny thought about ducking, but it was too late. The girl had spotted her already. And maybe it was a good thing that this little witch knew she was being watched. Amber looked at Henny, her face indiscernible, then she lifted her chin, an air of haughtiness. She jerked open her car door, climbed in, and sped away.

As Henny started her car, she wished Leyla were alive so she could ask why she wanted to pull her son away from Amber. Leyla hadn't struck her as a helicopter mom. Maybe she could talk to Prettie to find out more.

Amber was quickly climbing to the top of her list. Even if she hadn't had a hand in actually killing Leyla, she must've been connected somehow. The fingernail. Her jealousy. Her demeanor when they met at the sheriff's office. Something wasn't right.

It was possible that she was simply one of the many rowdy teenagers who partied at Sprigg's abandoned gas station, which would explain how the fingernail had gotten there. Jill also could be one of the kids who partied at that location. Or both of them. That fingernail could've been lost weeks ago and might not even be connected to the murder at all. But what about Amber's behavior? Was she just a typical moody teenager acting out? It was highly likely that her issues with Jill were just another day in the life of teenage drama. Henny turned toward home. She couldn't focus on any of this right now. She needed to get home to make the cake for the wake tomorrow and get supper ready.

17

Henny baked the pumpkin spice cake with a maple frosting. She sat down to a supper of chili and grilled cheese—a perfect complement to the dropping temperatures and blustery weather—and flipped on *Family Feud*.

The door in the kitchen opened. "Hello!" Cash called out.

"There's chili and grilled cheese on the stove if you want it."

"Awesome." After some rustling around in the kitchen, Cash came into the living room and flopped down on the couch with a grunt. He grabbed his laptop from the coffee table, the screen lighting his face.

Henny turned down the volume on the television. "You found a place to live yet?"

He scooped some chili into his mouth, nodding. "I think so. I have my eye on a place."

"Yeah? Where at?"

"Huntington Place."

"I don't know anything about it. Where is it?"

He chewed his food. "Across the tracks on the north side."

"Wait. Is that the one down the road from the quarry?"

"Yep."

Henny cringed inside. *Ew.* That wasn't a very good place, if it was the one she was thinking of. "Is it...safe there?"

"Safe enough, I guess."

She shook her head, stirring her chili. He was a grown man and needed his own space. If only he could get a good-paying job, he'd be able to afford a better place. "Do you have the money for the security deposit?"

"Yeah. They only want the first month as a deposit. Most places I've seen want first and last month deposit." He took another bite of food and typed, searching and pecking at the keys with his two index fingers. His phone pinged. He picked up his phone and read it. "And I think I found someone to room with, so that will help with the money."

"That's good. What about the job at Haisha Corporation?"

"I got a call today, My interview is in a few days."

"Tomorrow is Leyla's wake. Are you going?"

He tapped on his phone screen with his thumbs, then put the phone down and took another bite of chili.

"Hey. I'm talking to you."

Cash looked up at her questioningly. "Hm?"

"Are you going to Leyla's wake tomorrow?"

He scraped the last of his chili into his spoon and shoved it in his mouth. He spoke through his food. "Oh, yeah. Probably." He typed again on the laptop. His phone pinged again. He read his phone and texted something.

"What's going on over there? You sure seem busy."

"Nothing. Just, uh, making some arrangements."

"What kind of arrangements?"

"Why're you so nosy?"

Fine.

A silence fell between them as Cash typed on his phone, then on his laptop, and Henny watched TV. An ad for a Bacon Master popped up on TV. The size and shape of the bacon-ator reminded her of the missing object in her collection room. She turned to Cash. "Hey, I got a question for you."

"What's that?" He drank from his iced tea.

"I noticed earlier an empty spot in my collection room. It's about the size of a shoe box." She spaced her hands about a foot long. "About yay big..." She switched to about four inches wide. "And yay wide. Does anything like that ring a bell to you?"

He watched her hands and scoffed. He stood and swept his phone in front of him. "You see all this stuff you have in this house, right? How on earth would I know what you're missing? And, for that matter, how would *you* know?"

Irritation clawed at her scalp. "Well, for your information, Mr. Smart Aleck, there's a shelf in my room with a clean spot and dust all around it. So, clearly, something is missing. I've checked the room and don't see anything matching the size of the hole. I thought you might know something about it."

"Sorry. Don't know. I've got to go. Thanks for the chili." He closed the laptop and, leaving the empty bowl on the coffee table, strode out of the room.

"Where're you going?"

"Out. Don't wait up." The door in the kitchen slammed.

Aggravating man. And he'd made her miss all of *Family Feud.* She glared at the TV as the local news came on. "Might as well watch this. Find out what's going on." She turned up the volume.

The anchor, a handsome young man in a suit, sat behind a desk. He had shiny dark eyes, black hair, and a neatly trimmed beard. He said, "Tonight the sheriff's department is looking for information leading to the arrest of the person or persons involved in a gun-store robbery a couple of nights ago in Woodford County. Jackie Granger has more."

The petite reporter with a blonde ponytail and makeup thick enough to plaster a wall came on screen. She stood in front of a store with boarded-up windows. "Good evening. Two nights ago, around two in the morning, robbers smashed through the store-front of Nate's Gun Shop in Woodford County..." She turned to point to the building. It was a tan building with a sight-target symbol behind the name NATE'S on the illuminated sign over the door. Henny's mouth dropped open, and she pointed at the television. She'd seen that symbol before—on a tag she'd found out at Sprigg's garage. She wished now she'd kept it. Surely, the po-lice found it in their investigation. She refocused on the television.

"Located behind me." The reporter faced the camera. "The thieves stole at least thirty guns. Though there was a camera on the exterior of the building, it appears to have been inoperable on the night of the robbery. Cameras inside the store captured three people, stealing everything they could in the smash-and-grab." As the reporter spoke, a grainy black-and-white video showed a white car crashing into the store, sitting there for a few sec-onds, then backing out. Then three people, dressed all in black and masked, smashed glass cases to take everything they could grab and ripped guns off the wall displays, dropping everything in large canvas bags.

Even Henny could see there was no way to identify the rob-bers dressed like ninjas in a dimly lit room on a grainy camera.

Jackie the reporter returned. "The sheriff's department is asking for the public's help in identifying the car or the people. If you know anything at all about this crime, you can report anonymously to the Woodford County Sheriff's Department by calling the tip hotline." The number came up on the screen along with still shots of the car and the thieves.

Henny scooted forward and stared at the television. The car looked awfully familiar. In fact, if she didn't know any better... She squinted harder as if it would make the answer pop into her head.

Then it hit her. *Oooooh, no!* Couldn't be. Could it? There was no way Leyla would've been involved in a crime. Maybe she was... Henny shut her eyes, almost too afraid to think the thought forming in her brain. She must've been dead already. Was she already in the trunk at that point? Or being held somewhere?

She dialed Sheriff Basham's cell phone.

He answered, "Basham." There was the noise of a restaurant or bar in the background.

"Hi, sheriff. This is Henny Wiley. I'm sorry to bother you. But I've been watching the news tonight and saw something about that smash-and-grab at Nate's Gun Shop in Woodford County."

"All right."

"Well, on the footage, it looked like the car used was Leyla Hager's car."

He paused. "Are you sure?"

"About eighty percent. It looked an awful lot like her car. Wouldn't hurt to look into it."

"That explains some things we discovered in the investigation. Is there anything else?"

"Yessir. When I was out at Sprigg's that day when Leyla was discovered, I saw a Nate's Gun Shop tag out there, too. Along with a bunch of bullet casings. I figured it was a just a bunch of teenager nonsense, but now I'm not sure."

"Okay. If my deputies thought those things were important they would've put them into evidence."

She was anxious to know what else had been discovered, but she knew it was futile to ask. "I just thought you should know so you can talk to the police over in Woodford County."

"Thank you, Mrs. Wiley. If you have any further information, please feel free to call."

"I will." She hung up and rubbed her face. This was all too much. The sense of powerlessness was overwhelming. Her hands began to itch, and a fluttering filled her body limb to limb—the all-too-familiar sensation that preceded a dumpster-dive. She looked around her room at the boxes and the bags, the piles of newspapers and magazines, the knickknacks. *Resist.* She shut her eyes and squeezed her fists, fighting to resist the desire, like a demon threatening to overtake her. But with her eyes shut, all she could see was the look of disgust and pity in Mrs. Lopez's eyes. She didn't want that Lopez woman to fine her or take away her home, put her in assisted living or whatever other things the state did to people these days. She wrung her hands. Henny needed a distraction.

She stood, closing the footstool on her recliner, and headed toward the kitchen to grab her purse and keys. But, halfway across the floor, she stopped, noticing a blinking light from the couch. Cash's laptop. She played Solitaire on it yesterday. Maybe she could play for a little while. Only long enough to distract herself, to make the thoughts go away, to kill the desire to dumpster-dive.

18

At Prettie's house, Ida Mae parked her Buick on the side of the road, near the neighbor's driveway. Ida Mae carried a warm dish filled with chicken hashbrown casserole and Henny carried her pumpkin spice cake covered in maple caramel frosting as they tried to hold their skirts against the cold wind. They picked their way through the horde of cars packed in the driveway and along the sides of the road.

At the far side of the property, Cash stood in the road with Luke, Amber, and another young guy who looked identical to Amber. He had a dark, neatly trimmed beard, and a knit cap. He was the same man she'd seen Amber with in the parking lot recently. They all scowled, serious and furtive. Henny pursed her lips with a head shake of disapproval. Cash was way too old to be hanging around those kids more than half his age.

Ida Mae cut her eyes at Cash. "Is he still driving you crazy?"

"You know he is."

"Has he found a job or a place to live yet?"

"He seems to have some leads, but nothing seems certain."

"Well, I hope he finds his way out of your hair soon. Look at him. He just looks like he's up to no good."

They sighed in unified frustration with their brother as they stepped up on the porch. Henny and Ida Mae entered the house and greeted Prettie, her delicate form wrapped in a black sheath dress and pearls. After a while, Luke in a black suit and Amber in a floral burgundy dress entered the house, holding hands, their noses and cheeks pink from the cold air. They made their way to another corner of the room, removed from the group.

After all the guests had arrived, Pastor Steve said a brief prayer, and everyone formed a line at the buffet established on the long cherrywood dining-room table. Henny made a plate for Prettie alongside her own and took a seat beside her on the sofa in the living room.

"Here you go," Henny said, handing her the paper plate loaded with chicken hashbrown casserole, southern green beans, and broccoli salad.

"Oh, thank you," Prettie said as she accepted the plate and rested it in her lap. She poked at her food, pushing it around on her plate instead of eating.

Henny patted Prettie's shoulder as she scanned the room. "Leyla had a lot of friends."

"Oh, yes." Prettie nodded with a weak smile. "She was always the popular one. So outgoing. She was the homecoming queen in high school. Went to the prom every year. Was Miss Kentucky one year. She made friends everywhere she went. I was always the quiet, nerdy one with my nose in a book."

They shared a smile.

Henny's attention fell on Amber, and she recalled what she'd heard from Jill about the tensions between Luke's mom and girlfriend. She said, "This might not be the best time to talk about this. But I heard something recently..." She took a bite of green bean casserole. "About Amber and Leyla. I'd heard they didn't get along very well."

Prettie didn't seem to mind the topic. "They didn't. In fact, Leyla hated Amber so much, she was actively trying to break them up."

"Really?" Henny watched Amber hanging on Luke's arm. "Do you know why? Did Leyla ever talk about it?"

"She wasn't crazy about Amber's family. Apparently, her brother was always in trouble. In and out of jail. And she thought Amber's parents were...weird." She set her plate on the coffee table and toyed with the wadded tissue in her hands. "She said she couldn't pinpoint what it was about Amber and her family, but she always said there was something *off* about them." She lifted her glasses and dabbed the corner of her eyes. "And she didn't like Amber's control over Luke. Amber says *jump* and he says *how high?* Leyla didn't think it was healthy." She drank from her water with a lemon wedge floating in it. "The final straw for her was when Luke said he didn't want to go to college even though he had a full scholarship for football. He said he wanted to go to the community college instead because that's where Amber was going to go until she transferred to an out-of-state school." She sniffed a half-laugh. "Leyla hit the roof. And you know Leyla. She was never shy about telling you what was on her mind. So she had a talk with Amber."

"How did that go?"

Prettie shook her head. "Not very well. Amber went to Luke and pulled him into it. So he was caught in the middle of them, trying to please them both. Amber played him like a fiddle and drove a wedge between him and his mom." She sighed. "It wasn't pretty. But Leyla was stronger-willed than either kid had anticipated. She kept pushing, and I thought Luke was beginning to come around until..." She looked down at her hands.

Until Leyla died. Henny cut her eyes at Amber, who pulled Luke over to a corner away from all the other guests. Boy, looks could be deceiving. To look at her, Amber seemed sweet, gentle, even mousey. But in recent days, Henny's eyes had been opened. Amber's controlling, bullying behavior belied her appearance. Which led to another concern: to what extent was Luke involved? Surely, he wouldn't have lifted a finger to hurt his mother or conspire to hurt her. Yet, if Amber really did have as much control over him as Prettie claimed, that could be problematic. She watched Amber lean against Luke and wrap her arm around his shoulder, making it plain who he "belonged" to.

The doorbell rang, and someone standing nearby opened the door. Marcia, dressed in a black rockabilly dress, stepped inside. Her black hair was pinned in a bun, and she wore a lace shrug over her tattooed arms. Her face was pale, dark eyeliner, and her lips shaded a deep red. Carrying a box of cupcakes, she stepped across the floor to Prettie, who stood to greet her. "Hi, Prettie. I brought these for you and Luke."

"Thank you, sweetie."

Henny popped up. "I'll take them into the kitchen for you." As Henny walked away, she heard Marcia say, "I just wanted to pay my respects..." By the time Henny returned to her seat, Marcia had moved over to Luke, who stood to greet her. They hugged, and Amber stared ahead with blank eyes and a tilted smile.

Henny and Ida Mae spent time with Prettie, listening to stories about her memories of Leyla as they all laughed through tears. After several glasses of iced tea, Henny turned to Prettie. "Where's your restroom?"

"Oh, down the hall, the last door on the right before you reach the stairs."

Henny pushed through the crowd and entered the bathroom decorated in silver jacquard wallpaper and pale-blue accents. When she had finished her business, she turned out the light and opened the door. To her left was the wake, and to her right were the stairs leading to the upper level. She glanced to the left again. What if she poked around in Luke's room or Leyla's room for a bit, just to see if there was anything interesting to the case? She pulled her phone out of her minipurse and texted Ida Mae. **I'm going upstairs. Don't let anyone up here.**

Ida Mae texted back **Don't you dare! You're going to get us in trouble.**

I don't have time to argue with you. This is for Cash!

Ida Mae sent back an angry face emoji.

"Whatever," Henny muttered, tucking her phone into her minipurse. She turned to the right, glancing over her shoulder to ensure no one was following her, and tiptoed up the carpeted stairs. She quickly peeked through rooms, finding a guest bedroom, a bathroom, a closet, Prettie's room, then Leyla's room. Leyla's room was neat, orderly, and decorated in shades of turquoise, copper, and cream. Henny wasn't sure what she was looking for, but was certain she'd know it when she saw it. She rushed into the room, closing the door behind her, and set about looking through every drawer she could find, including the jewelry box, and she searched the closet. There was nothing of any significance, as far as she could tell.

Henny cracked open the door, peeked out, and, seeing all was clear, stepped into the hall. She made her way to the last room—Luke's. She opened the door, peeked inside, cast about one more glance, and closed herself inside the room. It smelled of active teenage boys—sweaty clothes and Axe cologne. His room was, in short, a pigsty with clothes, shoes, and books strewn everywhere. Football posters covered his walls, and stacks of video games littered the space around his television. She could spend a month trying to find clues in this mess and wouldn't be able to. Henny didn't have that kind of time.

She turned to leave and noticed a purple bag with white handles under a pile of dirty athletic clothes. That looked just like the one in Cash's room. She pulled the bag out from under the pile and knelt down to unzip it, when she heard the door open behind her. Luke and Amber looked down on her, Amber angry, Luke confused.

"What are you doing?" Amber said, storming into the room.

Henny jumped up, embarrassed at being caught. "I-I-I noticed this bag." She lifted it up. "It looks just like the one in my brother's room."

"I don't know where that came from. It's not mine. But why are you in my room?"

Amber snatched the bag from Henny's hand. "Give me that. It's *mine*."

"I-I-I'm so sorry," Henny said, her mind racing to grab onto any feasible explanation. "My brother has a bag just like it and it surprised me. I was wondering how his bag got into your room."

Hurt twisted Luke's features. "I didn't steal his bag, if that's what you're implying, Mrs. Wiley."

"These bags are pretty common," Amber said. "Tons of people at Plumridge High have one." She turned it around to show the school logo. "The real question is why your brother has one. He probably stole it."

Henny was fully aware of her brother's criminal past, but she didn't like outsiders saying anything about it. She grew warm with a rising anger. "Now, hold on a hot minute, missy—"

Marcia appeared in the doorway. "Hey..." Her eyes widened when the trio turned to look at her. Amber glowered at her. Marcia continued, smiling at Luke: "Uh, sorry to interrupt, but, Luke, your dad is outside and wants to speak with you. Prettie asked me to come tell you."

"I'm on my way." He turned to Henny. "You should probably go now."

"Of course, I'm sorry." He and Henny turned together toward the stairs. "I was...confused," she continued. "Please forgive me."

"It's okay. Just get out now."

They went down the stairs.

"How long has the bag been in your room?"

"I don't know. Like I said, I didn't even know it was there."

"So, it really is Amber's?"

"Must be. It ain't mine. Mine is a Nike bag."

"Why's she keeping her bag in your room?"

"Beats me."

"Has she done that before, left stuff in your room?"

"Sure. We've been dating since last summer."

They reached the ground floor and passed down the hallway. Luke stepped outside, and Henny returned to the living room.

Ida Mae rushed to her side. "What in Sam Hill do you think you're doing?"

"I wanted to try to find some clues."

"Did you find anything?" Ida Mae crossed her arms over her chest.

"I found a purple duffle bag identical to the one in Cash's room."

"Okay. So?"

"You don't think that's odd?"

Ida Mae thought about it. "Maybe. What was in it?"

"I don't know. I got caught before I could open it, because *someone* wasn't paying attention."

"I was too! Who caught you?"

"Luke and Amber."

"Well, I was watching. There are a ton of people here. Somehow they slipped past me."

"Let's go. I'm too embarrassed to stay."

The sisters said their goodbyes to Prettie and headed toward the door.

Suddenly a scream, followed by a series of heavy thumps, sounded in the house. Everyone stopped like antelope on the Serengeti sensing a lion.

"Where did that come from?" someone said.

Another person said, "It sounded like it came from down the hall."

Amber ran down the hall. "Hurry! Marcia fell down the stairs!"

A gasp went up, and people began to scramble down the hall. Henny pushed her way through as Amber pressed herself against the crowd and Ida Mae shouted, "I'll call 9-1-1!"

Henny and Prettie reached Marcia first. Henny grabbed the banister to assist herself to kneel. She tapped the girl's face. "Marcia! Marcia!" There was no response.

A few minutes later, all the wake-goers stood in the yard, watching the paramedics load Marcia in the back of the ambulance. People whispered and shook their heads. Luke stood with his hands in his pockets, kicking at something in the grass with Prettie beside him, her tiny bird-fist pressed to her lips and Amber on his other side, a strange look on her face. Henny stared at the girl, thinking she looked almost prideful or as though she was suppressing a sense of triumph. Henny couldn't prove it, but she knew that little demon-seed had something to do with Marcia falling down the stairs. For a second, Amber's gaze shifted to connect with Henny's. Amber cocked a brow, a thin Mona Lisa smile on her lips. Then she wrinkled her brow with concern and sadness, looked up into Luke's face, and linked her arm through his.

19

enny dragged herself to the house. It hadn't been a long day, but it'd been draining. Ida Mae honked as she pulled out.

Once inside, Henny fired up the coffee maker and cut off a slice of the chocolate cherry cake. She needed the boost. She thought about the wake, about Amber and Luke. Luke, that sweet boy, had nothing to do with his momma's death. But Amber was a viper. She recalled Amber's Mona Lisa smile as she watched Marcia being loaded into the ambulance. Amber must've had something to do with Marcia's so-called "accident." Then she remembered the purple duffle bag. Amber seemed really agitated over the bag. What was in it? Cash had been hanging around Amber and her brother a lot lately, too. It seemed more than a coincidence that his bag was the same style as Amber's. Or maybe it wasn't the same. She downed the rest of her coffee and pushed her way through the crowded hall to Cash's room.

There, in the floor at the end of the bed, was the purple duffle bag; it had the same logo as the one she'd found in Luke's room. She rushed forward and dropped to her knees to open it. Her hands shaking, she opened the bag to reveal a black face mask and a few guns with Nate's Gun Shop tags on them. "Oh, heaven help me! Cash, please tell me you didn't," she said to herself. She saw something gleaming silver in the bag and opened it farther. She knew she shouldn't touch it with her own hands, so she pulled the sweatshirt sleeve over her fingers and lifted the silver item out of the bag. A Mercedes medallion. Like the one from Leyla's car.

Ohnonononono! Not Cash! She threw the medallion back into the bag as if it seared her hand to touch it. Another spark caught her eye. Like glitter. She reached in the bag and lifted up the face mask. A few bits of silver glitter flecked the fabric. And it smelled of...she sniffed it...a sickly sweet scent like cotton candy and vanilla. Amber's perfume? She jerked the mask away from her face and returned it to the bag. "What do I do?" she muttered to herself. "Should I give this to the sheriff? If I told the sheriff, Cash would undoubtedly get in trouble too—even if he was unconnected to the items in the bag." Though, if he was unconnected, why was it in his possession? She needed to at least speak with her brother first. Maybe there was an explanation. She zipped up the bag and took it, tucking it in her collector's room until she could decide what to do about it.

Henny heard the kitchen door open and jumped to her feet. She rushed across the hall to close the door to Cash's room and to duck back into her collection room. She peeked through a crack in the door, watching Cash sidestep past the boxes in the hall and into his room. He left his door open. He was on the phone.

"Yeah. Okay. Sounds good. I just want to get the money and be done with it. Then I'm going on the straight and narrow. Got it. I'll see you at the old garage at midnight. Yep. Okay." He hung up his phone and tucked it in his pocket as he grabbed a bag from under his bed. It was a long, black canvas bag. He set it on the bed and looked around.

It was time to confront him. Henny picked up the purple bag and stepped into the hall. "Looking for this?"

Cash spun around. "Uh..." His brows knit tight over his nose. "Yeah, actually. But why do you have it?"

"Do you know what's in it?"

"No. I was holding it for Peter."

"Peter Knott, Amber's brother?"

"Yeah."

"Why?"

He shrugged. "Because he asked me to. As a favor. Said I wouldn't need to keep it for long. In fact, I'm taking it to him tonight."

"Taking it where?"

"You ask too many questions about things that don't concern you. Are you po-lice or something now?" He held out his hand. "Give me the bag."

Henny didn't move. "I know what's in this bag. Do you understand that if you were caught with this, you'd go to jail? Likely as an accessory for Leyla's murder."

"What are you talking about?"

She unzipped the purple duffle bag and opened it up for him to see. "The medallion from Leyla's car. A ski mask. Guns from the robbery of Nate's Gun Shop. This would go real bad for you, you dadburned fool."

His mouth dropped open. "I-I-I didn't know. I swear."

"Do you think the cops will believe that? Why can't you be friends with decent people? Why can't you *be* decent people? Momma and Daddy didn't raise you to be like this."

"I know!" He threw up his hands and sat down on the bed. "I know!" He dropped his face in his hands. "I want to be better.

I really do, but I..." He sat up and heaved a sigh, slumping. "I've always been the black sheep, haven't I?"

Henny steeled herself against his manipulations. She wasn't going to fall for it this time. "I heard your phone conversation. You're meeting someone at midnight? For what?"

"I'm going to give them these guns..." He patted the black canvas bag. "And they're going to give me money."

Her eyes widened. "Please tell me you didn't have anything to do with the robbery at Nate's."

"No! Of course not."

"Then where did those guns come from?"

"I'm holding them for Peter and his friends. That's all."

"Then how are *you* getting any money out of all this?"

"Just for being the middleman. For holding, transporting, and doing the sale."

"So, for taking all the risk..."

He shrugged again. "What do you want from me, Henny? I need the money so I can get on with my life and let you get on with yours."

"But not like this, surely."

"It takes money to get a home. To get a car so I can get to work. Then once I have a decent job, I can get on the straight and narrow."

Henny sighed and rubbed her face. "Why are you taking a risk for those guns? Are they even legal? Do you even know where they're from?"

"Not my business. I only care about the money." He stood and took the purple bag from her and zipped it up. "Look. I'm doing this one job, and I'll have enough money to start my new life."

"How much will you get paid?"

"Five grand. It would pay for my apartment and a down payment on a used car so I can take myself back and forth to work."

"I know five thousand is a lot of money. It is for me too. But you're risking everything, your freedom. Five thousand dollars seems too low a price for such a risk, don't you think?"

"You're right. But I have some other irons in the fire."

"Like what?"

A strange look she couldn't decipher came over his features. He looked away. "Just...things."

A car horn sounded outside.

"I've got to go." Cash stood and picked up the bags—including the purple duffle bag, which made Henny cringe. "I promise you, I'm doing this one job and then I'm done. I swear it." He stepped around her into the hall.

"Cash?"

He stopped and looked at her. "Yeah?"

"What about the purple bag? That has incriminating evidence in it. Don't you think you need to at least turn it over to the sheriff anonymously?"

The car horn sounded again. "I've got to go." He moved away from her.

"Just leave the bag here then, and I'll take it to the police."

"I'm giving it back to Peter. It's his bag, and he can do what he wants with it."

She sidestepped after him, her belly rubbing against boxes and bags. "Please, Cash. It's going to interfere with the investigation. It'll make it harder for the police to find Leyla's killer. She deserves justice. Give it to me. I'll take it to the sheriff anonymously. He'll never know you were involved at all." She caught up to him, grabbed the purple bag, and pulled at it. "Please. If the police know you had any dealings with this evidence, you'll go to jail for it."

"Henny, stay out of this." He pulled on the bag hard, jerking it from her grip. "I have my orders and have to follow them in order to get the money." He stepped out of the hall and pushed boxes into her path. "I'll be out of your hair soon. You should be happy about that much, at least."

"Dang it, Cash!" She tried to push the boxes out of her way and step over them as he rushed from the house. She shouted after him, "Please, Cash! Wait! Don't do this. There are other ways!"

The kitchen door slammed.

She growled. By the time she cleared the fallen boxes and made it to the door, Cash was gone.

Henny didn't know what to do. She slammed the door and put on the kettle for hot tea. "What on earth am I going to do now?" She should probably report him to the sheriff, but he was her *brother*, her flesh and blood, *family*. Henny didn't have much family left. She couldn't think of anything right now. She needed some mental space to get some clarity.

With hot tea in hand, Henny sat on the couch and opened the laptop. She would play some computer games and clear her mind. Perhaps by morning she would have a better idea of how to proceed.

Instead of the blue background screen with the icons, there was Cash's email account. As she searched for the X to close out the screen, she noticed the words "pawn," "price," and "Oz" in the preview panel. Her interest piqued, she clicked on it and opened up the email. It was from Palace Pawn in Georgetown. It read:

I looked at the Oz figurine box you brought to me and have done some research. I think you'll be happy with the price. It's from the Lenox Company, and the authentication cards are in the acrylic box you provided. Since everything is in good condition and authenticated, I can give you at least three grand for the set. Let me know.

Henny's heart dropped into her stomach and foamed like a bath bomb. Her figurine case! She had several sets of figurines, but those were the ones Walter had given her for Christmas one year. She had carefully placed the Dorothy and Toto, Tin Man, Scarecrow, and Cowardly Lion figurines in a protective acrylic box with their authentication certificates under their bases. The box had started out in their bedroom, then moved to the collection room on the top shelf; then, as more figurines and collectors' items had come into the house, she moved the box lower and lower until it had landed on the bottom shelf. It's not that she'd forgotten about it exactly, but that in the past few years other items in the room had covered over and hidden the bottom shelf.

And, apparently, Cash had taken it to this Palace Pawn and was going to sell it! Her own brother had stolen from her, had taken her beloved Oz figurines!

She paused to check Cash's response. Maybe he'd had a change of heart. Maybe he could be redeemed.

Cash's response was:

That's perfect. I'll be there before you close tomorrow.

She looked at the date. That was yesterday. That lowdown, stinky, sleazy skunk sac!

"What?" She shouted. This couldn't be real. She sidestepped down the hall toward her collection room as fast as she could push herself through. She wished she could move faster. She threw open the door to the collection room and flipped the light on. At first, nothing appeared to be missing. But as she entered the room and began inspecting the shelves, she noticed several empty, dust-free spots. The lunchbox. The dolls. The music box. The plate holders stood empty. A slew of her most cherished and prized *Wizard of Oz* items was gone. Deflated, she flopped down on the edge of the bed, her back pressed against a stack of boxes and plastic containers. "Oh, no." She sat, her shoulders slumped, and dropped her face in her hands. She wanted to cry, but she was too tired. She was nothing more than a husk of herself.

How could he betray her like this? A rage, heavy and cold as a stone, dropped into her gut as she dragged herself back into the living room. She slammed the lid down on the computer and shouted, "Walter, you were right about my brother! I'm sorry I didn't listen!"

Walter popped into the living room. "What's the matter, little lady?" he said in his best John Wayne imitation.

"He betrayed me." She choked back sobs. "He stole my treasures and was trying to sell them."

Walter stood, slouched, his face drawn with sadness and pity. "I'm sorry, Henny. I didn't *want* to be right about him."

She dropped her face in her hands and cried. "I've tried with him; Lord help me, I've tried. I was trying to be a good sister. Trying to help him when he needed it most, hoping he'd changed. I feel like such a fool. Clearly, I'm the only one who cares about keeping the family together."

Walter sat next to her. She could tell he'd put his arm around her because of the strip of cold that shot across her upper back.

"I'm sorry, hon. I wish I could give you a big ol' hug."

"Me too." Walter's hugs had always been the best. She missed them the most. "Just please don't say I told you so."

"I won't. I hate it for you. Truly. And, if I could, I'd wring his neck. Sometimes, Henny, your heart is just too big and you're willing to think the best of people who don't deserve it. Then you get hurt."

She wished she could lay her head in Walter's lap. She tried, but hit a pillow on the couch instead. She stared at the piles of magazines and newspapers on the coffee table, the thoughts and feelings swirling so quickly in her brain that it made her numb all over.

Walter added, "He's all kinds of wrong. He used you and took advantage of you. But that's the thing about people like him. They know you're kind and they'll use it against you. It's hard for people like you to understand people like him. And it's worse because he's your brother. You want to help him and pro-tect him, and it's hard to believe your kin is a bad apple. But he is. Rotten to the core."

Henny hung her head and nodded, wiping at the tears. There was hope. Always. Cash could still be redeemed, and she hoped he would be; she'd keep that hope tucked away in her heart like a secret. But his redemption wasn't going to come at her expense. She was done. The more she thought about it, the angrier she became.

20

enny shot up from the couch and grabbed her cordless phone from the table by her recliner. She was going to fix Cash's little red wagon. She called the Palace Pawn shop. When a man answered, she said, "This is Henny Wiley. Cash Cooper is my brother. He recently attempted to sell you a *Wizard of Oz* item, four figures in an acrylic box, which is *mine*. Do you still have it?"

"Ma'am, I don't have the items. He brought them by to have them appraised, but he hasn't turned them over to me yet. We were supposed to settle up later."

"Well, don't you dare purchase from him. That stuff is mine. He stole it."

"Is that so?" The tone in his voice turned dark and stormy. "I should've known. He told me they belonged to his dead mother."

That rat. "No, they belong to me. His very much alive and ticked off sister. What time do you close?"

"Fifteen minutes."

"I'm on my way." She hung up the phone and flew from the house. Only a sliver of daylight lit the horizon, casting the landscape in the dusky purple of twilight. She arrived at the pawnshop within ten minutes. She stepped into the store to face a tall man with a thick gold chain and dark glasses. He was moving around the store, preparing it to close. "Has Cash Cooper shown up yet to sell you my *Wizard of Oz* stuff?"

"No, ma'am." He turned to put a velvet tray of rings and other jewels in a safe behind him.

As her eyes tracked the glittery jewels, her mind turned to Leyla. "Has he sold you any jewelry recently? Because that's stolen too. From a dead woman."

"No. He never said anything about jewelry."

Henny relaxed some. Maybe that meant he didn't have the jewels. The guy behind the counter checked his watch.

He was closing; Cash hadn't come. "Thank you for your time." She returned to her truck and sat there, watching the pawnshop, waiting for Cash to show up with her *Wizard of Oz* items until the clerk closed up the store. She wanted to be sure.

While she waited, she called the sheriff.

"Basham," he answered, sounds of talking in the background.

"This is Henny Wiley." She paused. Moths fluttered against the lights in the parking lot and bright lights of cars swooshed by. Even in her angry state, she didn't feel good about directly snitching on her brother. So she needed to spin it. "I have two things to tell you. First, you need to be looking hard at Amber Knott and her brother, Pete, for the robbery at Nate's Gun Shop in Woodford County and possibly Leyla Hager's murder. Also, I'm pretty sure Amber pushed Marcia down the stairs at Prettie's house."

"I'm at the hospital with Marcia now, as a matter of fact. She's stated as much. I'm looking for Peter and Amber now."

"Well you might find one or both out at the old Elmer Sprigg gas station at midnight tonight. I heard there's going to be some kind of meetup there."

"Oh, yeah?" The tone in his voice sounded both interested and skeptical. "Involving what? And who exactly?"

"That, I don't know. But I think it has something to do with those stolen guns from the Nate's Gun Shop smash-and-grab the other night."

"How would you know that?"

"I overheard a phone conversation. That's all I'm going to say on the matter."

"Then how do I know this is a legitimate tip?"

She'd had enough of all of this. "Look, you either want to do your job or you don't. I'm offering you information I think is good."

"How do you know it's good?"

She shouted. "I can't tell you that!" And hung up the phone.

Henny flew back home. Her phone rang. *Basham*. She cut the call and turned off her phone. The black velvet of night had now fully wrapped up the tiny town of Plumridge, Kentucky, snug and cozy. Lights shone out from houses, and the scent of hickory smoke from fireplaces hung in the air. The moon and stars hung on the naked fingers of the treetops like the glittering jewels at the pawnshop. It'd be a beautiful night, perfect for a dive, if she wasn't so ticked off at her brother.

She whipped her car into her driveway and stormed into the house, muttering to herself. She sidestepped down the hall to Cash's room.

Walter appeared, sitting on the edge of the bed. "Whatcha doing?"

"I'm doing what I should've done days ago." She found Cash's luggage in the corner of the closet, pulled all of his things out of the closet and the drawers, and shoved them into the bags. She grabbed up shopping bags, dumped their contents onto the floor, and filled them with her brother's belongings. She then carried everything to the front door and tossed them out in the yard. She marched back to the kitchen, found paper and a pen, and scratched out a note:

> Your stuff is in the front yard. Don't ever come
> back here, you backstabbing weasel!!!

She underlined "backstabbing" five times and taped the note to the screened porch door at the back of the house.

The desire to run from the house and lose herself in the depths of a dumpster was overwhelming. Yet, over and over, all she could think of was Mrs. Lopez and the sheriff standing in her living room, all high and mighty, making her feel small and dirty. But the lure of the dumpster, all the treasures, the *treasures*! It pulled on her, sang out to her like sirens in the dark ocean depths calling out to sailors in the storm. She opened her hands and closed them into fists, over and over, kneading her emotions and thoughts like dough. She needed to resist the desire to rush from the house and find comfort in her favorite dumpster. She shook in resistance. *No!* She needed to take care of business first. She needed to make sure Cash wouldn't take advantage of her again.

Walter watched with interest. "What now?"

She seethed, pacing in little circles in the living room. Walter whistled the tune to "The Bridge on the River Kwai."

"Would you stop that dadburned whistling?"

"Doorknobs!" Walter shouted.

Henny stopped. "What?"

"Doesn't Cash still have keys to the house? If so, you need to change the locks."

"How do I do that?"

"Uh, changing the doorknobs."

"I don't have any doorknobs. Do I?"

"Yep. I found some out in the shed this morning."

"Why were you in the shed?"

"I like hanging out there sometimes."

She headed to the kitchen door to slip on a pair of yellow Crocs and grab the shed keys from the junk drawer. She stepped outside, with Walter floating behind her. The night air was frosty and alive with cricket song.

She marched across the backyard to the shed, unlocked it, and pulled the chain to turn on the light. It smelled of fertilizer and oil and was packed with plastic containers, boxes, garden and lawn equipment, buckets, empty flowerpots, bags of soil and mulch. She sidestepped through one of the narrow paths. "I can't remember where I put them."

Walter said, "They're under the workbench in a box."

She knelt down and sorted through the small boxes and finally found the brand-new doorknobs. "Here they are."

"You're going to need a screwdriver, too. A Phillips head, and a utility knife to open that blister pack. Check my toolbox on the bench."

Rummaging through the box, she found the tools she needed. She and Walter returned to the house. She stood there with a utility knife, looking at the blister pack containing the new doorknob.

"What's wrong?" Walter asked.

Henny blinked and breathed heavily. "I don't know. I-I can't open the package."

"You haven't even tried."

"No: I mean, I don't think I want to open the package."

"You have to if you're going to replace the doorknobs."

"But I might need these someday." A fog descended over her mind, veiling her thoughts, weighing them down.

"Henny, darlin', you need them *now*."

She searched Walter's ghostly face. She was well accustomed to that look of confusion, pity, and annoyance. "Yeah, but—"

"No, Henny!" His voice grew stern. "You need to do this, and you need to do it now or Cash will come back. He will use his keys, come into the house, and you'll never get him out. Then what happens when he takes your treasures? He'll take them all and sell what he can."

Henny shook off the mental fog. "You're right. You're right." She sliced open the blister pack and removed the components. "I have to do this," she muttered to herself. "It's for the best. It really is."

Walter talked her through installing the new doorknobs. She locked the doors and shut them and put the new keys on her keychain, wiping her tears on the shoulder of her sweatshirt. The job completed, she paced in front of the television, wringing her hands. All she could think about was Cash, his betrayal, and her missing *Wizard of Oz* treasures.

The Betrayal!! She kicked a stack of papers and books. Out of the middle of the stack fell a latch-and-hook kit. The box was yellowed and wrinkled and flattened from years of being squished in the pile. The image on the box was a red barn, baskets of pumpkins and apples, an old-time red truck, and the word HOME in large letters across the top. She picked it up.

She hadn't seen this in ages. She'd bought it at a yard sale, back when Walter was alive. It reminded her of the farm they'd once had together, so her plan had been to make that into a rug for the door as a warm reminder of her life with Walter. Then she got distracted, then he was gone, and the rug never got made.

Sorrow hung on her heavily as though stones had been packed on her shoulders. Her head grew thick and throbbed, and pressure built up behind her eyes as if she might cry. She wished she could cry, wanted to cry, but tears wouldn't fall. It was as if the heat of her rage evaporated the tears before they fell. She rubbed her forehead and eyes to release the tightness building up. She could still make the rug, and then when her house was in order, she could put it by the door as a reminder of a new way forward.

She opened the box and pulled out the plastic bag full of brightly colored snips of yarn, a little latch hook, and a woven mat with the imprint of the picture on it. She pulled out the directions and looked at them. Soon, she was watching television, hooking little bits of yarn into the weave; and each time the thought of rooting through a dumpster bubbled up into her mind, she popped it with the latch hook and pulled it through the weave into a bright tuft of yarn. She worked feverishly, popping the thoughts one by one until they fizzled out into a quiet numbness.

21

Though her mind had stilled and the anger cooled, Henny could not let go of the fact that Cash had taken her *Wizard of Oz* things. She had to get them back. She checked the clock on the wall. *Eleven*. She had time. She could go out to Elmer Sprigg's abandoned gas station, confront her brother, and get her stuff back.

She wriggled out of her recliner and dressed in a warm jacket, gloves, and boots.

Walter appeared. "What're you doing?"

"I'm going to get my stuff."

Walter sat on the kitchen table. "You've got plenty of stuff here that's still brand-new, never been used."

"But these are *my* treasures. My *Wizard of Oz* things. I've been collecting my *Oz* stuff since I was a child. Some of those things were given to me by Momma and Daddy, Ida Mae, and you. I didn't get them out of a dumpster. They're important to me."

"Because we were important to you?"

"Of course."

"But those things aren't us, Henny. If you lose them forever, you still have us."

"No, I don't. Momma and Daddy are gone. You're gone. Mostly. The only one still here with me is Ida Mae. Those things are my ties to y'all. They keep the memories alive."

"Nonsense. Darlin', *you're* the keeper of the memories. Not those things."

Henny turned it over in her mind. He was right, but... She shook her head. "I understand what you're saying, and you're right." She shrugged. "But it's *mine*. He stole them from me. I love my *Oz* treasures, and I want them back."

Henny headed down the dark and winding Route 23 toward Elmer's abandoned garage. She checked the clock on the dashboard. *11:43.* Almost midnight. She needed to hurry. She pushed on the gas pedal and flipped on the bright lights, moths and bugs splatting against her windshield. Henny scanned the shadows for critters—especially deer.

There on the left emerged the ghost of Old Man Elmer's garage. She turned her truck into the lot, hoping she'd arrived before anyone else. She hoped the sheriff would come by to check out the tip she'd given him. But, honestly, she just wanted her stuff back. The rest, the sheriff could deal with.

When she pulled in, there was a silver sedan with dark-tinted windows, waiting. Cash stepped out of the passenger side. Henny left her truck running and got out. She pulled a giant, heavy-duty ice scraper from behind her truck seat and stormed toward him. "Cash Hollis Cooper. I want my *Wizard of Oz* stuff and I want it right now or so help me..." She let her voice trail off.

His eyes darted. "Henny, you need to get out of here. This is not a good time."

"I'm not leaving until I get my stuff or your skin. You choose." She pulled the ice scraper back, ready to wallop him right in the kneecap, wishing she had something sturdier that would hurt more.

"I'll give you your stuff, I swear. But you've got to leave. It's dangerous. You don't want to mess with these people."

She whacked him in the knee. He screamed and grabbed his knee. "Dang it, Henny! What'd you do that for?"

"I ain't playing with you, Cash. Where's my stuff?" She pulled back to hit him again. "I talked to the pawnshop guy and I saw your email. I know you're stealing my stuff to sell it."

"Okay, okay. Hold on." Cash limped back toward the car. The driver got out. She couldn't see him because his headlights were too bright, but she could hear them talking.

"What's going on," the guy said to Cash. "You want me to take care of it?"

"No," Cash said. "It's just my sister. Get back in the car."

The driver didn't get back in the car.

Another vehicle pulled in behind the silver car. The lights jabbed in Henny's eyes, and she held up her hand to shield her eyes against the light, which helped her make out that the vehicle was a large red truck with shiny chrome exhaust pipes. Peter Knott.

The truck shut down, lights and all. "Good night," Henny muttered, rubbing her eyes. "Why are car lights so blasted bright these days? We ain't trying to land planes." Car doors slammed. She heard voices.

She blinked at the cars, only able to see strange orbs in her vision. She heard "You!" then the sound of running feet and a shadow coming at her between the orbs, then *POW!* She was tackled and thrown to the ground, the ice scraper falling from her grip. The scent of cotton candy and vanilla cut off her breath as hands wrapped around her throat. "I'm going to end you."

Amber. Henny grabbed her hands and tried to tell her to get off of her, but she couldn't speak. Her breath came in sips as she clawed at Amber's hands and wrists and bucked her body to try to throw the girl off of her.

"Henny!" Cash shouted. She heard the shuffling of more feet. Cash loomed over them. He said, "Get off my sister." He wrapped his arms around Amber and lifted her off of Henny.

Henny coughed, gasped, and rolled to get herself away from the more immediate danger. She sat on her knees at the shadowed woodline behind the garage, coughing and getting her breath while Amber fought Cash like a little wildcat, screeching, kicking, clawing, and punching at him.

As Henny caught her breath and her vision returned, Peter Knott stepped up behind Cash and put a gun to his head. "Put her down. Now."

Henny patted and searched the ground around her, trying not to make noise. The scuffle had displaced her ice scraper. Where had it gone? She shielded her eyes against the headlights and searched the shadows. Old shopping bags embedded in wet leaves and mud, empty plastic bottles, rocks. *Dang it!* She needed some sort of weapon. Henny patted her pockets. *Ugh!* She'd left her phone in her purse. In the truck. She looked longingly at her truck, about twenty yards away.

Cash said, "She attacked my sister first, man."

"I just want to get this exchange over with." Peter paused. "Where'd she go?"

"Who?" Cash said.

"The old lady."

Henny scowled. *Old? The nerve!*

Cash said, "I don't know where she is. Can we just get this drop done and go our separate ways?"

"All right. Amber," Pete said, "go back to the truck."

"Petey—"

"I said go!" he shouted, his voice echoing.

"Fine!" Amber shouted and stormed back to the truck. She climbed up on the hood and sat there, fuming, picking at her nails and looking at her phone.

Though her knees screamed in pain, Henny duck-walked across the wet leaves behind a stack of tires and pallets, alongside the silver sedan, until she came up near the red truck. There was a rusted-out metal trash can lying on its side, filled with brush, and vines growing out of holes in its side. She picked up the lid and a glass bottle beside it.

Cash, Peter, and the other driver congregated around the back of the silver sedan. The logo on the back of the car looked sleek and elongated, like a running antelope or something. Was that an Impala?

The other driver was a short man with wide shoulders. "Put the gun away, man, before you shoot your foot off. Ain't nobody worried about that old lady. We'll take care of her before we leave." His voice was gravelly, like he'd spent a life smoking cigarettes and drinking whiskey. He popped open his trunk and said, "Here's what we've got."

They shined a light in the trunk. Henny stretched her neck as far as she could while remaining hidden, but she couldn't see anything. She did, however, get a good look at the unknown driver. He was lanky with longish, wavy hair. He had droopy eyes and a mustache like something out of a spaghetti western. Henny had never seen him before.

Pete studied the trunk, stroking his beard. "My guy said he wants those for sure. And maybe those, depending on the cost. He was pretty sure you could cut us a deal."

Mr. Mustache said, "What kind of deal? How much you got?"

"Fifteen grand for the whole lot of it."

Mr. Mustache snorted. "I don't think so, man. You'll have to do better than that." He took out a cigarette, lit it, and leaned against the car. He blew smoke. "I'll give you the guns for fifteen, but the rest of it stays."

Pete thought for a moment, arms crossed. He whipped out his gun on the guy and said, "Or we'll just take it all. Now. For nothing."

Henny's eyes popped wide and her whole body filled with adrenaline. In the distance, truck lights floated down the road.

Mr. Mustache stayed cool, staring at Pete.

Cash said, "Pete, man, what are you doing? Are you crazy?"

"Shut up, Cash," Pete said, his gaze locked on Mr. Mustache.

"Man, you're going to get us killed. If his people find out about this, we're done. We'll be worm food."

Amber watched with interest from her perch on the hood of the truck.

"Shut up!" Pete turned the gun on Cash, who threw his hands up and backed away. Then Pete focused the barrel back at Mr. Mustache. "I'm doing this, and you're not going to stop me. I'll bury you both right along with that nosy woman."

Henny frowned. *Nosy woman?* Was he talking about herself? Or about Leyla?

"Yeah," Amber snorted. "You can give Leyla my regards."

With all the talking, Henny wasn't certain, but she thought she heard the crunch of tires on gravel. From the far side of the building came Basham's voice, "Police!"

Everyone kicked into action. Amber slid from the top of the truck, hiding behind it. The men scattered like sparks from a bottle rocket as deputies poured around the other side of the building, shouting, weapons drawn.

"Get down! On your knees!" Basham shouted, pointing his weapon at Mr. Mustache, who tossed his cigarette and dropped to his knees. "Hands behind your head. On your belly."

Another deputy gave the same treatment to Pete; and another wrangled Cash, who was shouting "My knees hurt, I can't get down! You *know* me, Griff."

Amber crouched down behind the truck wheel. She inched toward the woodline. If she got into the woods, she'd get away. Henny wasn't about to let that happen. Henny eased to her feet, rubbed her aching knees, picked up the trash-can lid, and flung it at the girl like a frisbee, hitting her across the upper back. Amber spun to look over her right shoulder, just as Henny launched herself at Amber to crack her in the back of the head with the empty glass bottle. Amber was dazed, but still put up a fight.

"Help! Over here!" Henny shouted as they tumbled to the wet ground, rolling in the dirt and trash. Henny wrestled with Amber, trying to keep the girl's hands off her throat. She was mighty strong.

Basham ran over and trained his weapon and flashlight on Amber. "Freeze!"

Amber ignored him and continued clawing at Henny's face. "I will kill you," she shrieked.

"Backup," Basham shouted as he dove in to pull Amber off of Henny. Boots sounded on the pavement. Henny scrambled backward out of Amber's reach as two officers struggled to get control of the enraged cheerleader.

Soon, Amber, Pete, and Mr. Mustache were rounded up and put in the back of the paddy wagon. Cash, his hands locked behind him in handcuffs, was the last to be led away.

Henny stood by the wreckage of her truck, picking wet leaves and twigs out of her hair, her eyes filling with tears. No matter how mad she was at her brother, and even though he was a rotten apple, he was her flesh and blood. It still hurt to see him cuffed, knowing he was going back to jail. Her heart ached for him, for the fact that he couldn't seem to control himself enough to lead a productive and happy life.

Before he got in the back of the vehicle, he said, "Sheriff, can I have a word with my sister?"

"If she wants to speak to you." He turned to Henny. "Mrs. Wiley?"

"It's okay."

Cash said, "I'm sorry, Henny. For all of it. I'm sorry I stole from you. You tried to help me when I needed it most and I took advantage of you. I guess that makes me the scum of the scum."

Henny wiped dirt from her hands with a wet napkin. "It probably does."

"I know you're still mad at me. You should be. I'm not going to ask for your forgiveness right now. I know it's too soon. But I hope, someday, you can forgive me."

Henny's head throbbed: not just from the fighting, but from the emotion pounding at the inside of her skull. "Maybe. Someday. When you get out, come to my house...last."

Humor flickered briefly on his features, then faded as he nodded. "Fair enough. Maybe I can come sit for a spell...and a piece of pumpkin pie?"

"Maybe." A smile tickled at her lips, then died.

"Bye, Henny."

"Bye." She watched the officers lead him toward the paddy wagon. She didn't know when she might see her brother again, or even if she would. "Wait!" She rushed to him and hugged him as tightly as she could, as if it might be the last time she'd ever see him. He tucked his head against hers as a means of returning the hug.

"I love you, Sis."

"I love you too, Brother."

He stepped into the paddy wagon.

"Hey, Cash! Where's my *Wizard of Oz* stuff?"

As the door was closing, he shouted, "You'll get it."

22

The next morning, after a visit to Marcia at the hospital, Henny and Ida Mae picked up Cash's stuff from where Henny had thrown it into the yard and took down the Halloween decorations.

"Poor Marcia," Henny said, picking up the plastic pumpkin and black cat.

"It's a wonder Amber didn't kill her." Ida Mae unplugged the ghost inflatable and rolled it up.

"She sure tried."

They carried the items to the shed in the backyard.

"All because she was jealous of Marcia," Ida Mae said.

"There was more to it. She heard and saw things she shouldn't have."

They stuffed the Halloween items into the shed.

"True." Ida Mae planted her hands on her hips. "Let's gather Cash's stuff. What are you going to do with it?"

"I'll hold on to it until he can come get it, I guess."

The sisters gathered up the bags Henny had thrown out the night before and carried them to the master bedroom. They stuffed everything into a dark corner of the closet.

"No telling how long it'll sit there," Ida Mae said.

"Hopefully not too long." Henny sighed, pushed some boxes

out of the way, and closed the door. "Maybe he can get a deal. But it's here when he needs it."

"Let's get started on the living room."

"How about some coffee and cake first?"

Ida Mae smiled. "I know you're stalling. How about we start cleaning; then we'll take a coffee break in a couple hours."

Henny's shoulders tightened, sending flutters of anxiety into her fingers. She wrung her hands. The word "clean" meant throwing things away. Getting rid of things. Not having them anymore. She blew out a breath. She wasn't sure she could do it.

"We can do this," Ida Mae said, putting her arm around Henny's shoulders. "C'mon. One step at a time."

They made their way to the living room. Henny stood in the center of the room turning in a slow circle, her gaze casting over the boxes, papers, containers, bags, bottles, and knickknacks. "I don't even know where to begin."

Ida Mae picked up a box closest to herself. "How about this one?" She set it down on the coffee table and opened the flaps. She and Henny sat on the couch and peered inside the box. It was filled with boxes of new Christmas cards, ornaments, and other Christmas-themed decor, much of which still had the price tags on it.

Henny selected an ornament covered in red glitter. She turned it around and around, watching the glitter catch light. "Isn't it pretty?"

"It sure is. But how many ornaments do you have already? I know you have a bunch Momma and I gave you over the years. In fact, I bet you have enough to decorate five big Christmas trees."

"Maybe. But if one of those breaks, then I'll have this one. You never know when you'll need something."

Ida Mae studied her. "True, but you have a million replacements here. You can't keep them all. You don't want to get in trouble with the sheriff and that woman from Adult Services, do you?"

Henny sank, pondering it. "Maybe."

"What if we donated them to a shelter or the church, where they will get good use?"

Heat broke across Henny's back and shot straight into her chest, flashing up into her face. It was similar to a menopausal hot flash in its strength, but was different in its tone. There was an undercurrent of agitation with this one that didn't usually accompany her regular hot flashes. She wiped her forehead and fanned her sweatshirt. "It's getting warm in here." She stood and turned the ceiling fan on.

The doorbell rang. Henny rushed to open the door. Sheriff Basham, in his street clothes—flannel shirt, jeans, and cowboy hat—held a box.

"Hey, Sheriff," she said.

"Mrs. Wiley. I believe this belongs to you." He handed her the box. "Your brother asked me to return it to you."

She accepted it and looked inside. Her heart leaped. "My *Wizard of Oz* stuff! Thank you so much, sheriff. Won't you come in? My sister and I were just about to take a break for coffee and apple hand pies."

"We were?" Ida Mae said.

"Yes." She turned back to the sheriff. "My sister made apple hand pies straight from our great-grandma's recipe. Best you'll ever eat."

His hard eyes lit up. "Sounds real nice. I think I will sit a spell." He removed his hat.

Henny rushed into the kitchen, and Ida Mae followed close behind. Henny buzzed around making coffee, gathering plates and utensils. Ida Mae washed her hands and leaned over to whisper to Henny as she heated the pies. "You're stalling. I'm not stupid."

"Oh, hush up and clear the table."

Ida Mae cleared the table as the sheriff pulled out a chair and hung his cowboy hat on the chair ear.

"How's our brother?" Ida Mae asked, moving things off the kitchen table to make the clearest eating space possible.

"He's well. In a holding cell, waiting to talk to his defense counsel."

Henny set saucers of pie, along with forks and napkins, on the table. "What is he going to be charged with?"

"Tough to say. He was on probation, so that won't help. From what I can gather in the initial interview, he will probably pull down some kind of accessory charges."

Ida Mae set empty coffee mugs on the table, along with the cream and sugar. Henny filled the mugs with coffee. Then the sisters joined the sheriff at the table.

"I know you can't talk in-depth about the case," Henny said, "because it's an ongoing investigation, but can you give us *some* information? After all, our brother was involved somehow."

The sheriff pulled from his coffee. "Mm. Good coffee." He cut off a corner of his hand pie. "Welp, what I can say is Pete was selling stolen guns. Seems his sister would help hide the guns while he worked to find buyers."

"I think she was involved in the robbery at Nate's too," Henny said, chewing. "Cash was carrying a purple bag. In that bag was a ski mask with silver glitter and it smelled of cotton candy-vanilla perfume. All that points to Amber. She wore glitter when she cheered at games, and she wore that stinky perfume."

"I think so too," Basham nodded. "Though she hasn't admitted to anything yet. We're working now on gathering further evidence. DNA, fingerprints, fibers. All the usual stuff."

Ida Mae said, "What about Leyla? Is this all connected somehow?"

"Yes and no. Amber doesn't know it yet, but one of the guys has flipped on her to buy some leniency from the courts. She killed Leyla, in part, because she was afraid Leyla was going to force Luke to break up with her. Marcia's testimony points in that direction, as does Luke's. However, my intuition tells me that Leyla probably knew something about what Amber and Peter were up to. I think that information will eventually come out though the girl is pretty tight-lipped about it right now."

"She was one of the last people to see Leyla alive. And in the purple bag I told you about is the Mercedes hood ornament that's missing from Leyla's car." Henny sipped her coffee.

Ida Mae shook. "Oooh. Like a trophy or something."

Basham nodded. "Exactly."

"So why did Cash have the bag?" Ida Mae asked. "He wasn't involved in the robbery, was he?"

"I think she gave it to him to hold so she wouldn't get caught with it. Maybe she was going to frame him?" Henny said, looking to the sheriff for validation of her theory.

"It's entirely possible. Mm-mm, this pie *is* the best I've ever eaten." He shoveled another piece into his mouth.

"There's more where that came from," Ida Mae offered.

He wiped his mouth with a napkin. "No, thank you. That was plenty. But to answer your question, we don't think Cash was involved in the robbery."

Relief washed over Henny. "Thank goodness."

He continued, "We've been studying the video footage from the robbery, and it appears the robbers were younger, more agile, thinner than your brother." A light smile crossed his lips. "It appears that Amber and her brother were two of the suspects. We're looking for the third."

"I hope you find him." Uneasiness settled over Henny. "Please tell me Luke didn't have anything to do with his momma's death."

Basham swallowed his coffee. "Best I can tell, he didn't know about any of it. Amber had him completely hoodwinked."

"He has a bag in his room too," Henny said. "I found it yesterday at the wake. Right before Marcia fell down the stairs."

He nodded. "We found it. Amber had left it there, and being a teenaged boy who trusted his girlfriend, he didn't think anything else about it. It was soon covered up with his dirty laundry and athletic gear, and it sat there."

"She was probably going to frame him too," Ida Mae muttered.

"Probably. We did find a weapon connected to Leyla's murder in that bag. And in Amber's first interview, she's already been trying to throw our attention in his direction. She's a crafty one." He shook his head. "He was lucky she didn't pull him in deeper. Get married and such."

A lull passed between them as they finished their pie and coffee.

The jewels! Henny had almost forgotten about those. "What about Prettie Davis's family jewels? Did y'all find those?"

Basham relaxed against the back of his chair. "Nah, unfortunately. They're probably long gone, sold off to some pawnshop. We've sent out faxes and emails to the pawnshops here and in surrounding counties, and we put up an informational post on our social media. At this point, the best we can hope for is some Good Samaritan seeing something and reporting it."

"Poor Prettie," Henny said. It was hard to lose beloved things, things with history and sentimental value.

"Do you know who took them?" Ida Mae asked.

"I imagine whoever killed Leyla took the jewels too."

The sheriff checked his phone. "Well, ladies, I have a Honey-do list to attend to. If you'll excuse me..." He stood, pushed his chair in, and collected his hat. "Thank you for the pie and coffee. Mighty tasty." He stepped through the living room toward the front door. He opened the door and turned to Henny. "Mrs. Wiley, if you want any help with the cleanup efforts, let me know. Oh, and I wanted to give you this..." He reached in his pocket and pulled out a business card. "This is a therapist I know who specializes in this sort of thing. Reach out to her if you want to talk."

Henny hesitated, then accepted the card. "Thank you, Sheriff."

He clapped his cowboy hat on his head. "I'll be back in thirty days. I hope it'll be a visit as good as this one was. Ladies." He touched the brim of his cowboy hat and stepped across the yard to his truck.

Henny closed the door and looked around. *Thirty days.* "How am I going to get all this done in only thirty days?"

Ida Mae wrapped her arm around her shoulder. "It's okay, hon. You don't have to have it perfect. You'll only need to show you're making progress. Deep breath. Deep breath."

Henny nodded and inhaled a deep breath. "Okay." She exhaled. "Okay. Where were we?"

"Going through this box. I think we can donate all this. What do you say?"

"Maybe. Can we make a 'Donate' pile, an 'I Don't Know' pile, and a 'Trash' pile? And we'll put that box in the 'I Don't Know' pile."

"Fair enough." Ida Mae moved some things around. "This corner is the 'I Don't Know' pile. But we can't put *everything* there." She picked up a garbage bag and opened it. "Let's find one thing we can actually throw away or donate."

Panic flittered through Henny's mind. "I don't know. I don't think I can give up anything yet. So far, everything is important. I need it all. I've organized some things. That's progress. Right? A-a-and I put away my Halloween decorations and organized the stuff around my shed to make my nosy neighbor happy."

Ida Mae didn't seem convinced. She dropped the bag. "Okay." She looked around the room. "You know where I would begin throwing stuff away?"

"Where?"

"Right here, by your recliner." She held up an empty soda bottle and an empty Styrofoam food container. "You could start by throwing these away."

Henny blinked at her, silent.

"You understand why, right? They're empty food containers. You don't need them. You'll never need them again."

Henny continued to stare, opening and closing her hand as it began to itch. "Yeah, maybe."

"No, not maybe. In reality."

Henny's chest grew tight, and the room grew warmer. "I guess I could start there."

"Here, just drop it in. Easy peasy..." Ida Mae held the garbage bag open like a large white mouth. She handed the bottle to Henny.

Henny said, "You do it."

"Sorry, hon. It's important for you to do it."

Henny wiped her lips and took the empty bottle. She stared at it. Heat expanded through her body, and the itchiness in her palms spread into her skin, torso, scalp, and legs. It was as if a horde of ants was scurrying inside her veins under the surface of her skin.

"You can do it," Ida Mae said. "I know you can. You're strong. Do it for Momma and Daddy. And Walter."

Walter hovered in the corner of the room. "You can do it, Henny. I know you can."

Henny swallowed the lump of emotion surging in her throat. She stepped forward and dropped the bottle into the bag and jerked her hand away as if she'd been burned. Shaking all over, staring at the lump in the bag, Henny gnawed on her lower lip. She should probably retrieve the bottle. She could use it somehow. A container for her buttons or she could fashion it into a candle holder or a bird feeder. She scratched at the intense itchiness rising in her scalp. She stepped back from the bag and released a shaky breath.

Ida Mae and Walter hooted and cheered. "See! I knew you could do it!" Ida Mae said.

Henny released a faint chuckle. She picked up the empty Styrofoam container and shoved it into the garbage bag too.

ABOUT THE AUTHOR

Born and raised in the beautiful Bluegrass state of Kentucky, **MICHELLE BENNINGTON** developed a passion for books early on that has progressed into a mild hoarding situation and an ever-growing to-read pile. She delights in transporting readers into worlds of mystery, both contemporary and historical. In rare moments of spare time, she can be found engaging in a wide array of arts and crafts, reading, traveling, and attending tours involving ghosts, historical homes, or distilleries. Find out more on her website: www.michellebennington.com and follow her on Facebook, Instagram, and Goodreads.